The Shadows of Ghadames

The Shadows of Ghadames

◆◆◆◆

Joëlle Stolz

Les Ombres de Ghadamès
Translated from the French by Catherine Temerson

DELACORTE PRESS

Published by
Delacorte Press
an imprint of
Random House Children's Books
a division of Random House, Inc.
New York

Visit us on the Web! www.randomhouse.com/kids
Educators and librarians, for a variety of teaching tools, visit us at
www.randomhouse.com/teachers

Library of Congress Cataloging-in-Publication Data

Stolz, Joëlle.
[Les Ombres de Ghadamès. English]
The shadows of Ghadames / Joëlle Stolz;
translated from the French by Catherine Temerson.
p. cm.
Summary: At the end of the nineteenth century in Libya, eleven-year-old Malika
simultaneously enjoys and feels constricted by the narrow world of women, but an
injured stranger enters her home and disrupts the traditional order of things.
ISBN 0-385-73104-3 (trade) — ISBN 0-385-90131-3 (GLB)
[1. Muslims—Fiction. 2. Sex role—Fiction. 3. Literacy—Fiction.
4. Libya—History—19th century—Fiction.] I. Temerson, Catherine. II. Title.
PZ7.S875837Sh 2004
[Fic]—dc22
2003021656

Book design by Michelle Gengaro-Kokmen

Printed in the United States of America

October 2004

10 9 8 7 6 5 4 3 2 1

BVG

The Shadows of Ghadames

The Rooftop Race

My father left on a trip early this morning.

This is our way of life in Ghadames. The men are often away on the desert tracks while the women wait for them on the rooftops.

But since this morning I can't stay still. I wander around the house, worried and tense, like an animal that senses a great windstorm is on the way.

Bilkisu woke me up before sunrise from a sound sleep. I had been rolled up in one of my mother's worn, soft and cuddly wool veils. I think I was dreaming of caravans. . . .

"Hurry up, Malika, if you want to say goodbye to your father!" Bilkisu says.

It is dark but I make out Bilkisu's smile as she leans toward me, her heavy silver rings pulling on her earlobes. And, above all, I recognize her smell, so unlike my mother's, a blend of jasmine and peppery spices.

Bilkisu knows I have a superstitious fear of letting my father leave on a trip without saying goodbye to him. If I fail in my duty today, something dreadful could befall him.

"Hurry up," she says again more gently. "He's already in the kitchen, about to shut the grain storage container."

I scramble to the stairway leading to our rooftop. It is as straight and narrow as a rope ladder. I am so used to its steep incline that I can climb up even in the dark without falling.

Upstairs, I shiver from the cold—the desert cold at the end of the night, when not a single cloud protects human beings from the immense black sky.

Fortunately my mother has already lit a fire and sparks are flying to the corner of the roof. I like our kitchen, with its palm trunk beams worn by the smoke of the cooking pots, and its earthenware jars, covered with basketwork lids, for preserving food. And the convenient holes in the wall next to the hearth for the salt brought by caravan, one hole for the coarse gray cooking salt, the other for the fine white table salt that squeaks when you rub it between your fingers.

But, most of all, I like the grain storage container built into the corner farthest away from the fire; it is reassuringly potbellied, with a small round opening like a belly button.

"Good morning, my child."

My father greets me with a smile. His camel-hair burnoose is slung over his shoulders and his head is wrapped in a turban with the flaps floating around his neck. When it's time to leave, he will fold them over his mouth, as the Tuareg nomads do.

My mother does not look up. She is holding her measuring jar and counting in a low voice, taking out the amount of wheat and barley we will need for our meals during my father's absence. I hear the grain crackling as it rolls inside the wooden plates placed on the ground. Take exactly what's needed, that's our custom. We can feast and celebrate again only when the men return.

More than anyone else in Ghadames my mother, Meriem, insists on a strict adherence to traditional practices. I watch her in the glow of the fire as she divides up the grain and packs it down, with her fingers spread out. Her straight forehead, strong eyebrow line and delicate mouth are the features of a queen. She has bluish tattoos on her forehead and chin, and a mark in the shape of a star on each of her cheekbones. I know these tattoos have a magical significance, but I am not old enough yet for the women to explain it to me.

"Bilkisu," my mother says, addressing my father's second wife, "you can pour the barley into the large jar in the pantry."

Bilkisu picks up the plate. Though she never raises her voice, my mother has a commanding tone. Perhaps that's why I feel more at ease with Bilkisu, who treats me as though I were her own daughter. Bilkisu is tall and lithe, draped in indigo blue veils. She often laughs; when my father hears her, he can't help looking at her.

Her task accomplished, my mother lifts the plate filled with grains of wheat and holds it at arm's length. It is time

5

to hermetically seal our grain container. Before sealing the opening, my father removes any putrid fumes that may taint the grain by slipping a burning wick inside the container.

For a brief moment, the glow of the flame outlines his angular jaw and his aquiline nose, and I feel a violent pang in my heart. I realize how much I will miss him during this trip, more than ever before. He straightens up, throwing the thick pleats of his burnoose behind his shoulder. Then he looks at me, his intense gaze making me feel like a real person, not like a child whom people caress without seeing.

"Look after yourself, Malika, and take care of your mother."

He has never spoken to me like this before.

When we come out of the kitchen, the rooftops of Ghadames are cast in a pink light, their pointy, white-washed triangular corners jutting up in the sky. The slender crescent of the moon is barely visible, like a brushstroke in a lighter color above the palm grove.

"We live in a very ancient city," says my father softly. "Don't ever forget that."

I summon my courage. "Papa, please let me come with you to the entrance of the city. I really want to see the departure of the caravan. Up on the city walls you can hardly make out anything. It's too far away!"

"But you're just a girl! I am the one who gets to go

with our father," comes a voice. "Your place is with the women."

From behind us, Jasim's voice gives us a start. So he has finally gotten out of bed. He never leaves me in peace, always harping on the fact that I am "just a girl." It's his favorite refrain, and he whistles it between his teeth with a mocking air as soon as our mothers are out of earshot. "I am going to travel, I am going to drive caravans, I'll be going to Kano and Timbuktu, and all the way to Mecca and Istanbul! While you, you're going to stay right here and never go anywhere!"

But I know how to make him mad too. I contort my face in various ways without saying a word until he runs away. He is terrified by my grimaces. You would think I was no longer his sister but a creature come out of the darkness, a ghoul, a horrible ogress who eats children. But here, in front of my father, I don't dare make faces. And this morning, Jasim looks too much like his mother, with his mischievous eyes and his high, prominent, dark forehead. How could I get mad at Bilkisu?

"Since you are the two children God has given me," my father declares, "both of you will come."

I hardly have time to jump for joy before my mother reprimands me. She heard my father's pronouncement and I know she doesn't approve. A slight frown, a crease in the corner of her mouth, tells me her thoughts.

"Go downstairs and get dressed, both of you. Malika, your hair is a mess," she says.

I obey halfheartedly, and linger at the top of the stairs in the hope of hearing what she will say to my father. I know it's naughty, but I don't care. . . .

"Do you think that's good for your daughter?" my mother asks calmly, with no trace of anger. "Malika will be twelve years old this coming Ramadan. Soon, much sooner than you think, she won't set foot in the street anymore; our rooftops will be the only country where she'll be allowed to travel. That's the way it has always been for the women of Ghadames and that's the way it will always be. We'll only be giving her false hopes and pointless regrets, if you agree to take her beyond the city walls this morning."

I have never heard my mother speak at such length. My father is silent. Then he sighs.

"You're probably right. Twelve years old, already." He lowers his voice. "At that age, weren't you almost married, Meriem, to my great joy?"

I see my mother look up at him, smiling, and I go down the stairs quickly, my throat tightening as I hold back tears.

Bilkisu immediately understands. She is waiting for me, with a big wooden comb and a small jar of oil to use on my thick, curly mop of hair.

"Don't worry, Malika. You'll learn that we have our own way of traveling, and that it takes us much farther than the desert tracks."

"How is it possible to travel far without horses or camels, and without leaving the city?" I reply sharply.

Her eyes shine and she brings one of her long fingers up to her mouth. "It's a secret. Soon you'll know it. In the meantime, we'll still go to the edge of the city walls to see the caravan. Using the women's road."

I accompany my father down the stairs to the narrow entryway that gives out into the street. Jasim, glowing with pride, helps my father with his two large saddlebags. My mother and Bilkisu stand side by side. They have taken off their jewelry. Their bare faces, one lightly tanned, the other dark, blend with the design of red palm trees and flowers— the magnificent garden that all the women of Ghadames paint in red, on the walls of their houses, to protect them against misfortune.

Papa has been careful to place the oil lamp pointing inward in the niche. This way, if a visitor looks in through the hole in the door, he will immediately know that my father is off on a trip. Placed another way, or unlit, the lamp conveys a completely different message. For example, *The master is in the palm grove.* Or, *There has been a death in the house.* The men know not to knock at the door when, thanks to the little lamp in the entryway, they see that the women are alone in the house.

Before going out, Papa leans toward me and holds me tight.

"I'll bring you back a gift," he whispers, infuriating

Jasim, who thinks our father spoils me far too much since I am "just a girl."

Then they both slip away in the dark alleyway.

Mother does not want to come with us to the city walls. She is convinced that nothing bad can happen to my father as long as she is watching over the house at the precise moment when the caravan sets off. But Bilkisu doesn't share the same superstitions, and she is just as eager as I am to break up the monotony of our reclusive existence. So here we are jumping like goats over the small walls on the rooftops, our heads covered, but our dresses held above our ankles, so that we can walk faster and be the first to arrive by the women's road.

The rooftops of Ghadames are like a city above the city, an open, sunny town for women only, where they walk about, lead their own lives, visit one another, and never talk to men. Twenty feet below, the men walk in the cool shade of the alleyways, conduct business, and never talk to women.

These two worlds, my mother often says, are as necessary and different as the sun and the moon. And the sun and the moon never meet, except at the beginning and end of the night.

We almost break our necks during our wild stampede, but finally we reach the northwest wall, with its tall fortifications and square tower. Here, outside the city walls, the Iforhas— the tribe of Tuareg nomads who escort the tradesmen of

Ghadames to the far ends of the Sahara—have their encampment. The camel drivers have been waiting since dawn with at least twenty animals, all loaded with packsaddles and saddles, their forelegs hobbled, their mouths scornful.

At that instant I see my father's silhouette, with his honey-colored burnoose, and the blue djellaba that Jasim is sporting for the occasion. It's maddening that they're so far away from me! How can my father possibly recognize me among the identical veiled creatures perched on the city walls like a row of black birds?

I try to attract his attention by waving my hand, but he is too busy securing the saddlebags on the back of his camel. Gently, he makes the animal kneel down, then he eases himself onto the saddle, seizing its prominent pommel. Now comes the tricky moment—when the camel rises to its feet. As the animal stretches its front legs, one must be careful not to fall backward; then as the hind legs are raised, there's danger of sliding frontward, over the camel's neck! But for my father, all of this is second nature.

This will be his last caravan before the intense summer heat. He must go all the way to Tripoli, a twelve-day trek to the north, if he is to make a profit selling the ivory, gold dust and fine leatherwear that he brought back from Kano two months ago. It is already too late to travel south: the sun burns the men and their mounts, and the oases along the road are teeming with snakes and scorpions that were sleeping deep in the sand but have now awakened from their winter slumber.

Jasim hands my father the long rifle with the silver butt, and the bags of gunpowder and bullets. Occasionally the men have to defend themselves against robbers. After a final check to make sure that everyone is ready, and that no bundles have been forgotten or left on the ground, the camels set off.

I keep my eyes fixed on the disappearing caravan for a very long time, until it is no more than a dancing point in a halo of dust.

"Jaaasim!"

Bilkisu stands at the edge of the roof. Her cry plunges into the shade of the alleyway, bounces along the walls, and reaches the tiny square where my brother so enjoys playing with his friends. This concert of mothers—a symphony of male names called out in strident voices from the four corners of the sky—can be heard echoing from all the roofs of the city.

This is the hour when the sun turns red, the men prepare for the evening prayer, and the boys must come home. Bilkisu and our servant, the elderly Ladi, bustle about the kitchen preparing the evening meal. They were both born in Kano, the large city beyond the desert where the houses, like ours, have little horns—pointy triangular corners on the rooftops. Though they are completely fluent in our Berber dialect, when they are together they like to speak in their soft-sounding Hausa language.

Ever since this morning I've been going around in circles with no purpose, irritated by everything I see. The rooftop, with its view of the horizon that I will never reach, I find loathsome. And our entire house—with its palm trees painted on the walls in unreal colors, its imbedded mirrors that capture every bit of light coming from the outside, and its prints that my father brought back from countries that I will never see—seems like a cage, embellished so that the birds no longer want to fly away.

"What's wrong with you today?" Ladi asks me, puzzled upon seeing me so agitated.

But I avoid her gaze and dodge her dark-skinned hand, callused by work, as she tries to touch my forehead, cheeks and stomach to see if I am physically ill.

"I don't hurt anywhere, Ladi!" I say. "It's just that I wish I were somewhere else. I'm tired of having to stay here all the time."

She sighs. "Well, you can't do anything about that, nor can I."

I decide to open one of the cupboards, the one with green, yellow and red designs on its doors. We put away our food and clothes in cupboards because our bedrooms are so small there is only space for a few pillows.

But this cupboard isn't like the others. A freshly painted, white rectangle is concealed behind its doors. Here, using a piece of charcoal, my brother does his writing exercises with Bilkisu's help. Afterward you just whiten the wall and start all over again as often as you want.

I hate these lessons. My mother declared that I did not

need any and my father did not dare challenge her. When Jasim reviews his morning recitation from school, I escape to the rooftop and don't come down. Sometimes, I sit on the top step and try to follow my brother's lip movements and the shapes his hand traces on the wall. But I get the signs muddled when I look at them, as if a door I don't want to open anymore has been shut inside me.

When he comes home, Jasim finds me in front of the writing cupboard and I can't help blushing. He looks at me with a mocking little smile. I am about to retaliate with one of my deadly grimaces when, to my great astonishment, he makes a suggestion.

"Want to race on the edge of the rooftop?" he asks.

Well, that's quite an event! It's been at least two years since Jasim has completely stopped playing with me. He is interested only in his friends, and he lets me know it at every opportunity. Maybe he thinks I've forgotten how to run without falling? Or he hopes I'll fall, so I'll feel humiliated.

"All right," I say, "but if I win . . ."

My brother grins. "If you win . . ."

". . . you'll give me the board and stylus you use in Koranic school."

"And what would you do with them? You don't even know how to read."

"I am asking for them, that's all."

"Fine. Anyway, I am sure to beat you."

He dashes to the stairway ahead of me. By the time I join him, he's already perched on the low wall waiting for me. Naturally, he's chosen the easier, lower side that runs along the rooftop of the neighboring house. He left me the more dangerous side.

I am choking with rage. Maybe he thinks I'll beg for mercy! Without saying anything, I take off my embroidered slippers, so that I can better feel the top of the wall under my bare feet. I leap up and, like him, get my balance, but at the opposite corner. No one is paying attention to us. Aren't the children of Ghadames accustomed to walking on the edge of the rooftops from early childhood?

Vertigo makes my legs wobbly when I look down. On my left is a vertical drop of the wall. The street is two stories below. In front of me, the top of the wall is barely wider than the sole of my foot. Fortunately, the most dangerous section isn't very long. I bite my tongue hard to rid myself of any fear, then I remove my linen belt and tie it over my eyes like a blindfold. I fondle the dangling moon crescents on my earrings with my fingertips and whisper a short prayer culled from oblivion: "Oh help me, great goddess Tanit."

"Malika, what are you doing?" my brother yells, alarmed.

"I am going to show you that I can walk on the wall even with my eyes closed!" I shout back.

"You're crazy! You might kill yourself!"

◆◆◆◆

15

But I am already moving my right foot forward on the top of the wall and feeling its tiny bumps. I concentrate fully on the sensation of my bare feet stepping flat against the rough, warm, dried mud surface. I no longer have any fear of falling, as though invisible wings had suddenly sprouted on my back. Taking small steps, balancing myself with my arms spread out, I advance toward my goal. That's it, I've reached the other low wall, and am almost home safe. Just a few more steps . . . I am running now, until I hit the pointy, whitewashed triangular corner that marks the end of my route.

Tearing off my blindfold, I find that Jasim has stayed rooted where he was, paralyzed with terror at the thought that I might plummet. His dark skin has turned gray. As for me, my knees start to shake from fear after the fact.

Just then Bilkisu emerges from the stairway. One glance and she guesses that something unusual has happened. She runs up to Jasim, who tells her in a few words, then she comes up to me, knitting her brows, and hugs me. I feel the slightly sweet taste of blood and the painful burn where I bit my tongue.

I look up. "Bilkisu, who is Tanit?"

She steps back slowly. "Where have you heard that name?"

"I don't know. I must have heard it, but I don't know who she is."

"Tanit is a goddess from ancient times, I think, from before Islam," Bilkisu says. "Come along now, both of you, and don't you dare do that again! At your age you shouldn't be playing these kinds of games. You're too big now."

My brother said nothing more. But after dinner, he comes to my little room and hands me the board and the stylus.

"Take them. Anyway I no longer need them. Maybe one day you too will learn how to read and write."

The Fugitive

Something woke me from the depths of sleep. A cry? A call? Sitting up on the thin mattress that serves as my bed, I listen closely. Nothing. Nothing but the silence of the house and the inky darkness of night.

Then why have I woken with this oppressive sensation?

Bilkisu and my mother are asleep in their rooms, each separated from the common room by a curtain. Jasim is sleeping in the alcove, which is comfortably lined with woven mats and pillows and which we call the newlyweds' room. As for me, I got permission from my father to sleep in the little room where he keeps his books. It is located a bit higher than the others, up a stairway, and light comes in by a narrow window giving out on the street. Maybe the noise came from outside?

But, now, there is no noise. It must have been a bad dream, as I sometimes have when my father is away. He said he would certainly be back before the next full moon. Every night, from our rooftop, I watch the slim crescent grow in size and despair at its slowness.

◆◆◆◆

Resting my head on my elbow, I drift off to sleep again, but suddenly a cry startles me. This time I know for sure it is coming from the street. Bilkisu has heard it too, for her room is close to mine. She joins me by the windowsill, without making any sound. We can't see very much through the wrought-iron grille, except for some shadows in a haze of smoke from burnt-out torches. But we hear a stampede of bare feet treading the hard mud ground, as well as increasingly loud calls and swearwords. Someone is being pursued in the night. Is it a thief — a looter who has succeeded in entering our city in spite of the watchmen posted at the gates?

"Ahhh!" comes another cry, a cry of pain.

"They've wounded him," whispers Bilkisu. "Or else . . ."

"Or else?"

"He tried to escape by the unlit passageway and knocked his head against the beam!"

The hidden beam — a perverse trap invented by the people of Ghadames to catch their enemies. Some of the very dark alleyways are deliberately left unlit, and, at the level of a man's forehead, carpenters have placed a palm crosspiece under the low vaulting. The residents of the neighboring houses instinctively lower their heads, but a stranger who doesn't know the area can seriously hurt himself, especially if he is running.

Both Bilkisu and I are holding our breath, trying to guess what is going on down below. Have they caught him?

The group of pursuers is still stampeding, then the men seem to hesitate and retrace their steps. We hear muffled exclamations and deliberations. They set off in the opposite direction and the echo of their steps grows faint. Bit by bit silence returns.

"I am going out to look," Bilkisu whispers to me.

"In the street? In the middle of the night?"

"I don't care. I have to know what happened. Be very careful not to wake the others!"

She has such a light step that often I am only aware of her presence from her smell. On this occasion she has made herself as supple and silent as a black cat in the night. My mother and Jasim are still sleeping peacefully, or so I assume, when I hear the faint squeaking of the door hinges. What a scandal if our neighbors were to see Bilkisu in the street, her head uncovered!

Intensely worried, I tiptoe down the steps of the staircase and stop in the entryway lit by the oil lamp in the niche. Suddenly, Bilkisu pushes the door open. Someone is with her, a man she has to support so that he won't fall.

"Shhh!" whispers Bilkisu. "I found him on the ground in the passageway. He must be hurt."

I don't have time to protest. She puts her hand over my mouth, then opens the door of the shed where my father keeps his saddles, empty bags and tools. The room is always cool because it is at street level. Panting from the effort, Bilkisu manages to drag the wounded stranger inside and place him more or less comfortably on a pile of bags. As for me, I look on, unable to move.

"Bring the lamp!" she orders.

The light of the lamp is dim at the end of the night, when its supply of oil is nearly used up. But, still, we can see the dark clot of coagulated blood on the man's forehead. Bilkisu has obviously guessed right: he must have crashed headlong into the beam in the passageway.

"This nasty wound has to be cleaned," she says in a low voice.

"But, Bilkisu, what are we going to do with him? He may be a criminal."

"It's not much of a risk for us given the state he's in at the moment. I am going to clean his wound as best I can and tomorrow Meriem and I will decide what to do next."

"What about Jasim?"

Bilkisu is silent as she considers that problem.

"He is going to his uncle's early in the morning and there's no reason for him to enter the shed before then. By the time he gets back, we'll have found a solution." Then she adds, "In these matters, it's better to trust only women."

So here I am, the keeper of a secret only the women know. I am momentarily overcome with a guilty conscience at the thought of my father and it occurs to me that if he had been here, it would not have been up to us to act. He would have made the decision. Yet I feel vaguely proud of the cool-headedness shown by my brother's mother, her defiance of all the rules of decency requiring women to remain passive and obedient, and in their husband's shadow. But how will my mother react, she who is so exacting with regard to custom? This will be a terrible blow for her!

While I am mulling over these thoughts, Bilkisu has had time to fetch some clean water and a bit of olive oil to rekindle the lamp. With better lighting, she can now dab the stranger's forehead with the tip of a piece of cloth. The white fabric darkens immediately and the man moans softly.

"This is a good sign," Bilkisu whispers. "He hasn't fallen into the deep sleep that often brings you to death's door."

With small, gentle gestures, she cleans the wound on the forehead, massages it briefly with oil, and covers it with a strip of clean cloth to keep out the dust. We can't see the stranger's face very well, but we see that he is young and has a dark beard. His eyes remain shut during the entire operation. Finally Bilkisu stands up again and spreads a blanket over the wounded man.

"Go back upstairs to bed. The sun isn't up yet."

I feel myself collapsing with exhaustion, my eyes prickling from the strain of making out her barely visible gestures in the half-light.

"And what about you?" I ask.

"I'll stay awhile and watch over him, then I'll go upstairs and light the fire in the kitchen. Don't worry and try to get some sleep. You were of great help to me."

◆◆◆◆

Everything happened just as Bilkisu predicted. I went back to sleep, exhausted, and Jasim left at daybreak without noticing anything unusual. The most difficult thing still remained: facing my mother. How could she ever accept sheltering a stranger in her house in my father's absence? Worse still, a man whom the city residents had pursued, no doubt for good reason?

Bilkisu must have decided that it was best not to conceal the presence of the stranger in our shed for too long. She took the precaution of waiting for Ladi's arrival, and for her own peace of mind, immediately sent the servant to fetch water at the spring. Then she woke me up.

"Come. It is time to tell Meriem."

My mother is preparing tea and looks impassive as always.

"What's wrong with you two?" she asks. "What happened last night?"

"So you heard?"

"I thought someone opened the front door. But then I thought it might be a dream."

While Bilkisu describes the events of the night, I see my mother's cheeks turn pale and her mouth become tense.

"You're crazy," she murmurs. "Crazy. The family's punishment will be horrendous. We may both be disowned."

"Is it a crime to come to the aid of a wounded person?" says Bilkisu. "Mahmud wouldn't send us away for that."

My mother sighs. "No, maybe not. But he will be mad at us for dishonoring him in front of everyone."

"Madame Meriem, we'll make sure that no man in the city finds out about it."

"But how? If he dies here . . ."

"Then we'll carry his corpse, at night, back to the passageway where he was knocked out. Who would ever see a link between this stranger's corpse and our house? If he survives, he'll walk out of here on his own two feet and we'll find some way of getting him out of the city."

My mother looks at her in a kind of horrified admiration. "You're so self-confident, Bilkisu. Where did you learn these things?"

"Instinct tells me that this is how we must act or else we're lost."

To my great surprise, my mother stands up and adjusts her veil. "You're right," she says. "First we must see if this man is still alive. Let's go downstairs."

He is still alive. In the semidarkness of the shed, where the half-open shutter lets in a ray of grayish light, we can see the wounded man's chest slowly rising and falling. He seems to be asleep, but occasionally his hand stirs, and he clutches his bloodstained gandourah. He looks like one of our people.

After having looked at him, my mother gathers her courage.

"We can't leave him here," she says. "We must carry

him up to the rooftop, to the storeroom next to the kitchen. And call Aïshatou; she will know how to nurse him. The sooner he heals, the sooner we'll be rid of him."

Aïshatou is a tall woman, with very dark skin, who is reputed to know many secrets. Some people say she is a bit of a witch, but we often call on her to treat wounds or illnesses. I am frightened at the thought of letting her come into our house.

At that very moment Ladi knocks at the front door. Two knocks of the door knocker always means a woman, and the woman can only be our servant since the other visitors always use the rooftops. Bilkisu hurries to relieve her of the heavy earthenware jar she is carrying on her head. My mother has prudently pulled the door of the shed closed to hide the wounded man. Ladi doesn't seem surprised to find all three of us on the ground floor, though we usually remain in the upper stories of the house. She is much too excited.

"Strange things happened in our city during the night! It was the main subject of conversation at the spring," she says. "The men of the Aïssaouïa brotherhood chased a man, hoping to drive him out of Ghadames. They say he is the son of a local family who went to study in the northeast and has returned to preach for a new brotherhood that is very powerful over there. But our people do not want to hear about it. They ordered him to leave or obey tradition. We have enough religious groups in this city, they say, with no need to create another one."

28

Bilkisu interrupts her impatiently: "What happened to the man they were chasing? Did they catch him?"

"That's the most extraordinary part!" exclaims Ladi. "They did not catch him! He disappeared into thin air . . . as if he went through a wall. Perhaps he was a genie, a ghostly spirit who took on the appearance of a human being to deceive us?"

My mother, who is afraid of *jinn*, or spirits, turns white. She exchanges looks with Bilkisu.

"Come," says Bilkisu to Ladi, taking her by the arm. "I have something to tell you . . ."

She continues in their own language. From Ladi's exclamations and her alarmed glances in the direction of the shed, I see that she doesn't approve of Bilkisu's boldness. But what is the point of challenging her mistresses' decision? She will not betray us. Ladi belongs to another brotherhood, which has many followers among the women of Ghadames, and there is no reason why she would want to help the Aïssaouïa, which admits only men.

Carrying the wounded man to the rooftop, up those steep and narrow stairs, is not easy, but between the four of us we succeed. He can't walk at all anymore, his bandaged head rolls from side to side, and he groans every time we pull him by the shoulders to hoist him up.

Finally when we manage to lay him down in a corner of our pantry, Ladi removes two large baskets of dates so that we can make a bed for him on the ground. The room isn't large, but it is well ventilated thanks to two small skylight windows fitted with wooden shutters. Bilkisu immediately sets off to find Aïshatou, who lives in another neighborhood, north of the city.

As for me, I stay near the man. My mother has taken a seat outside the doorway and has started to grind today's portion of barley, for here we say that grinding flour ahead of time brings bad luck. She is crushing the grains between two stones, making a squeaky noise. It is one of the many sounds that punctuate our daily life, like the hammering of the big wooden pestles with which the servants reduce date pits to a powder fed as gruel to the goats.

Occasionally she looks up from her work and glances boldly at our wounded man. Now we can finally see him in daylight: he is a very pale young man, with well-etched features. We can't see the color of his eyes, but his beard, hair and eyebrows are jet black. I can't help finding him handsome and I wonder whether my mother would agree. But I once heard her get indignant when she heard a woman talk about a man's beauty, so I decide to keep my thoughts to myself.

Suddenly, there is a shadow at the doorstep. It is Aïshatou!

She is even taller than I remember and as broad as a tower. Her skin is so dark that it looks bluish around the temples. Whether she is young or old, it is impossible to tell. She has hardly any wrinkles on her forehead, and her eyes are a surprising light brown—the golden color of certain leathers—but she knows so many things that she could easily be a hundred years old. She is wearing big silver bracelets that fit snugly around her wrists and make her powerful hands, with their nimble fingers, look even bigger. Her hands are the hands of a healer or a killer, I think with terror.

The tall woman greets my mother, then bows as she crosses the threshold to the pantry. Instinctively, I step back against the wall.

"Don't be scared," she says, smiling. "I don't eat children. At least, not yet."

Her smile broadens. She is making fun of me! Furious, I decide that from now on, I won't show any sign of fear in front of her. I will remain impassive, come what may.

"In fact you're no longer a child," she adds, looking me over with a penetrating glance. "If you don't mind please go stand on the rooftop, because I take up a lot of space and the poor man will have trouble breathing with both of us present."

I back out of the room, putting on my most dignified air, the queenly air that so irritates my mother. But Aïshatou isn't the least impressed; she has already turned her back on me and is leaning over the wounded man. With expert gestures, she raises one of his eyelids, feels his neck, and checks his heartbeat in the inside fold of his elbow. Finally, she removes the bandage from his forehead. First she inspects his wound very carefully, then the color of the cloth that was covering it.

"Bring me fresh water," she says without turning around.

When I return with a brass ewer and basin, she extracts a small leather pouch, softened from years of use, from her ample dress, and takes out a faded cloth sachet. The sachet contains a brownish powder that she pours into the palm of one hand. Then, with her free hand, she traces mysterious signs into the powder. So it is true that she is a witch? In spite of my resolutions, I prefer to sneak away and join my mother, who is waiting for the diagnosis in silence, sitting very straight in her blue-black veil.

She draws me to her bosom, and I recognize her fragrance in the folds of her dress, a blend of honey and warm biscuit. Now I remember! One day, a long time ago, as I was snuggled against my mother, I could smell her very distinctly, and I recall a tall woman next to us who was tracing signs with her finger in some flour on the ground, muttering incomprehensible words.

Tanit! The mysterious name that had popped into my head while I had been racing on the edge of the rooftop— I am certain I heard it then. And the tall woman was Aïshatou.

Finally here she is, coming out on the rooftop, bending down. Even when she sits cross-legged, like us, she towers above us majestically.

"I don't think he has fractured his skull," she says, "but at this point I can't guarantee that he will live. I've administered a powder on the wound that will prevent the flesh from becoming infected. If he wakes up before this evening, you should have him drink two cupfuls of the medicine I prepared in the brass pot."

"And what if he doesn't regain consciousness?" asks Bilkisu, who has come nearer.

Aïshatou opens her powerful hands, palms facing upward. "It will be God's will."

"I hope you understand . . . ," says my mother hesitantly.

"Don't worry," says Aïshatou. "I won't tell a soul about his presence here. It will be a well-kept secret. But beware too, Meriem!"

"What do you mean?" my mother asks, troubled.

"You will be tested," says Aïshatou in her deep voice, looking at my mother as if she could see through her. "But you have no reason to be afraid."

With those obscure words, she takes leave and walks away. I watch her silhouette for a long time, gliding from rooftop to rooftop, becoming smaller and smaller on the horizon, until it disappears behind a wall.

The wounded man regains consciousness before sunset. I am the first to notice because I am in charge of watching over him. My mother and Bilkisu rush in from the kitchen as quietly as possible, careful not to attract the attention of the neighboring women at the hour when they are preparing the evening meal.

He finally opens his eyes—his very dark eyes—and

looks around in vain for something familiar. But all he sees are three strange women in a room cluttered with earthenware jars, baskets and food supplies.

He tries to speak but is too weak; no sound comes out of his mouth.

"I am the one who found you last night in the passageway," says Bilkisu. "Don't worry, nothing bad will happen to you so long as you're in our house."

The young man nods, looking exhausted. He shuts his eyes once again.

"We'll let you sleep, but first you must drink this medicine," Bilkisu says firmly, pressing a cup against his lips. It contains some of the liquid prepared by Aïshatou.

He closes his lips tightly and opens his eyes again. What if this were poison? What if we wanted to kill him? His eyes roam over us anxiously, then settle on me. I smile at him encouragingly, and suddenly he relaxes, drinking from the cup Bilkisu is holding. He seems to have decided to put his fate entirely in our hands.

Abdelkarim

It is true that the stranger's fate is in our hands. The Aïssaouïa men are on the lookout for him. They don't believe he disappeared into thin air and wonder who helped him escape. This is what our uncle, an influential member of the brotherhood, tells us when he accompanies Jasim home that evening.

We did not expect his visit. Usually when someone is traveling, even the men of his own family refrain from entering his home when the women are by themselves. But this uncle is my father's eldest brother. He has authority over our entire family, and, because of his age, his presence here will not give rise to gossip.

My mother and Bilkisu lead him into the reception room, the most beautiful room; the cupboards are decorated, the floor is covered with rugs and pillows, the mirrors have vermilion designs around them. We are especially proud of our brass vases; we have dozens of vases with long necks that are lined up on shelves, extending nearly all around the room. When the morning sun lights up the walls, the vases shine like gold. When their surfaces tarnish, it's like a lamp turning off. The women spend hours polishing them! These brass vases represent the fortune of every self-respecting family, and we would have to be reduced to dire poverty before ever selling them.

My uncle accepts the lemonade we serve him, and then launches into the usual subjects of conversation: births, marriages, funerals, the next date harvest and the price of camels. My mother and Bilkisu listen to him with respect, sitting unobtrusively off to the side. They are both dressed simply, unadorned of any jewelry, as is proper for women of Ghadames whose husbands are far from home. In a word, they are irreproachable.

We sense that Uncle has something to tell us but does not quite know how to broach the subject. He beats around the bush for a while, praising Jasim, a good boy who shows an aptitude for commerce.

"He helped me at the store all day, and I really have no complaints," Uncle says. "Jasim knows how to read and count, and soon my ledgers will hold no secrets for him. Mahmud can be pleased to have such a son."

My brother puffs up with pride on hearing this praise. Uncle sighs.

"Oh, some families would be happy and thankful to have a son like him, thankful instead of being ashamed . . ." he says.

My mother arches her beautiful black eyebrows. "Whose family are you thinking of, Uncle?"

Uncle turns glum. "Don't you know what happened last night?" he asks. "The whole city is talking about it. And you women, up there on the rooftops, are usually the first to spread the news. You usually know everything well before we do!" He looks at the stairway as though expecting to see someone suddenly appear there. "Well before we do!" he repeats.

Bilkisu puts on her most innocent air. "Actually we don't know much. We were told that there had been a chase in the city, and in fact I was woken up, as was Malika, by all the noise they made down in the street. What exactly happened, Uncle? Whom were they chasing?"

"A man called Abdelkarim, a no-good son from the Beni Ulid clan whose parents died many years ago," Uncle explains. "When the boy was orphaned, he was sent for his education to a distant relative who lives in Cyrenaica. Since he showed an interest in religious matters, they thought he should become a *taleb*, a learned man who would open a good school here. But he fell into the clutches of the Senussiya, the brotherhood that wants to conquer the Sahara just as it has conquered Cyrenaica. According to them, we must return to the purity of Islam at the time of the Prophet and fight against superstitions! What they call superstitions are simply our traditions, as old and respectable as our city. These young people lack piety and respect; they think they can teach us lessons. But we immediately made it clear to him that he wasn't going to lay down the law here. Let him go preach elsewhere!"

"You mean he came back here to preach?" asks my mother softly.

"He came back a month ago and turned down his cousins' hospitality," replies Uncle. "Instead, he went to live in a little room outside the city walls, where servants and visiting strangers stay. Disgraceful behavior! He started stirring up young people against their elders, explaining that the true meaning of religion had been forgotten and that they alone had the energy to restore it. But I am keeping you for too long talking about things that don't interest women." He looks at each of us. "So you say you saw nothing last night? Because we lost his trail not very far from here, and though we've searched high and low, we haven't found him. No one knocked at your door last night?"

"No, Uncle, no one knocked at our door last night," says Bilkisu quietly.

All three of us know that she is telling the truth. Even if it isn't the whole truth, of course.

Having apparently put his mind at rest, Uncle is about to rise from his seat. Then Bilkisu brings up something else.

"Since you're here, Uncle," she begins, "I'd like you to know of a change concerning Jasim. He's grown up now, and it really isn't appropriate for him to continue coming to the baths with me, or to play on the rooftops in the company of women. That time is over. He showed you today that he is becoming a man, you said so yourself a minute ago. Since his father is away, for the time being Jasim will have to go to the baths with you. Do you approve of this decision?"

The old man has no choice but to agree. Yet he seems annoyed. Perhaps he had asked my brother to look around the rooftop to make sure the fugitive wasn't hiding there? Now there is no way of checking, and he has to take our word for it. Bilkisu's decision is final and he knows it; any boy who would disregard it would bring on himself the censure of all the women of Ghadames.

Just then I look at my brother. He has tears in his eyes and is trying very hard not to cry. It is all over for him. No more games of leapfrog on the rooftop, no more hours spent watching the flight of birds, or crouching behind the pointy horns of the roof and gaping at the neighbors' daughters! No more naps in the shade of the dresses drying on the clothesline. No more laughing fits at the baths, or sheen of naked skin as the women wash each other. No more wild races along the edge of the roof! Our race the other day will have been the last one . . .

Just as there is an age at which girls have to give up the amusements of the street and the palm grove, there comes a day when boys have to give up the pleasures of the rooftop. For Jasim, that day has come. Yesterday I was fuming about being confined to a tiny world; now I suddenly realize that for my brother, the rooftop will always be a lost paradise.

After accompanying our uncle down the stairs, Bilkisu

takes pity on Jasim, who looks sullen and lies prostrate on the cushions. She opens a cupboard, the one where we put away the pastries until evening during the Ramadan fast.

"Here, I baked some almond horns for you, to celebrate your first day working in your uncle's store," says Bilkisu. "I knew he would be pleased with you. That's why I also asked your father to bring back a nice present for you from Tripoli. I won't tell you what it is. I'll let it be a surprise."

Upon seeing the delicate cakes coated with shiny honey, Jasim's face lights up with a smile. His sorrow vanishes instantly. After all, life has many exciting things in store for a boy.

"Oh, I wish Papa were back!" he says with a sigh.

"Me too!" I echo.

My thoughts are with the wounded man and I am full of anxiety. What will we do about him? Still, I admire Bilkisu's cleverness in preventing my brother from having access to the rooftop. Now there is no danger of his sticking his nose into the pantry. No one else but us, along with Ladi and Aïshatou, will know that the fugitive is up there.

The following morning, Jasim, resigned to his new way of life, goes off to Uncle's store for the whole day again. His days at school are over as well. He has to become familiar with the ins and outs of commerce and the harshness of long-distance travel. My father talks of eventually sending him to Istanbul to stay with one of his associates, so that he will have the experience of seeing the world and crossing the sea. At one time, he thought of placing him with the Moslem wise men of Kairouan, but my brother shows very little interest in religious issues. He would be bored, he says.

And my brother is afraid of the sea. He finds it hard to imagine such a huge expanse of water, and how you can sail on it without being swallowed by the waves. I wish I could be in his place, I wouldn't be scared!

As soon as I wake up, I race up to the rooftop to see how the wounded man is doing.

"He is sound asleep," says Bilkisu, who is keeping an attentive eye on him.

Today, again, my mother doesn't dare enter the little room and is sitting in front of her loom. This is the wisest thing to do—not change our habits in any way so as not to attract our neighbors' attention. For here, without seeming to, every woman watches the others and someone may be surprised to see us prowling around the food pantry. Fortunately, the location of the door is such that it is impossible to look inside the house from the surrounding rooftops. And as long as we speak in low voices, no one can hear a word of what we are saying.

"Do you think he is going to die?" I ask.

Bilkisu shakes her head. "No, I don't think so. He is breathing regularly and his wound seems to be healing. But look at the state of his gandourah, with all the blood he lost! It is even starting to smell. It should be washed. Help me take it off him."

"But, Bilkisu, we can't undress a man! It isn't proper!"

"Bah, when a man is wounded, he must be helped. Don't worry, we won't take off all his clothes. He'll still have his undershirt."

I help her slip the long tunic very gently over the young man's head and arms. But in spite of all our efforts, the movements wake him up. He sits up suddenly, with a furious look in his eyes.

"What are you doing?" he protests.

"Calm down," replies Bilkisu. "We just wanted to take off your gandourah so that we could wash it. Look—there's a lot of blood on it from the wound on your forehead."

The young man instinctively raises his hand to his forehead but is still angry. If his dark eyes were flames, we would surely be reduced to ashes!

"Take off my gandourah! Who are you, to dare touch me?"

"My name is Bilkisu and this is Malika. But I won't tell you our family name. It's safer for all of us if you don't know it. I found you two nights ago in the passageway. You had blacked out. Do you have any recollection of that night?"

The young man frowns, straining to remember.

Bilkisu starts talking again, gently. "Aren't you Abdelkarim, of the Beni Ulid clan? The person the Aïssaouïa men want to chase away because he preaches for a rival brotherhood?"

The wounded man's face relaxes slightly. He stares at

the soiled gandourah, with brown stains, that Bilkisu is holding in her hands.

"Now I remember. I thought I'd get away from them by diving into the darkest passageway, but I forgot that there are often beams across them. This isn't my neighborhood and I was running at random. When I hit myself, it was terribly painful, but I did not faint. I heard my pursuers' footfalls. So God gave me strength. Leaning on the frame, I was able to hoist myself between the two walls and huddle on top of that beam while they searched for me in the darkness. They were there, so near to me, not even two inches below, but unaware of my presence. God did not want them to catch me! It's a sign that I was chosen!"

His face lights up, and his eyes burn even more than ever, but with a strange intensity.

"You were also lucky that I went down into the street to see what had happened and that I managed to carry you home," Bilkisu points out quietly, tilting her head slightly. "God did not make you any lighter to carry."

While we are talking, my mother slips into the pantry, wrapped in her veil. You can see only the oval of her face, her almond shaped eyes under the perfect line of her eyebrows, and her forehead devoid of ornament.

"This is Madame Meriem, the first wife and Malika's mother," says Bilkisu.

The wounded man scrutinizes each one of us thoughtfully. Then he addresses Bilkisu again.

"You've both taken off your jewelry. So, your husband is away on a long trip. And you dared to bring me into his house in his absence?"

He seems sincerely indignant. I see my mother blush with anger and her lips tighten. Bilkisu adopts a gently ironic tone of voice.

"Do you think it's appropriate for you to complain?" she says. "Have you thought about where you would be right now if we hadn't helped you? Abandoned in the desert, covered with blood, with no water or mount."

"Women should never act on their own initiative, without consulting a man who has authority over them," says the wounded man. "All too often they are guided by the devil."

His comments do nothing to disconcert Jasim's mother.

"You may well be a wise man who is never guided by the devil," Bilkisu says. "But didn't you spend time in a woman's womb before being brought into the world?"

Blood rushes to the young man's pale cheeks. He glares at her for her impudence. He opens his mouth, then shuts it. He prefers to remain silent rather than face another cutting reply.

For several days, he remains offended. It is as if we had committed a crime not just against him, but against the entire male population. I am the only one he talks to from time to time because I am in charge of bringing him food. Bilkisu and my mother keep away from the pantry, and it is all for the better, because that way there is nothing suspicious or abnormal about their behavior.

As always, they perform most of their tasks on the rooftop, working at the loom, washing the laundry, grinding the flour for the evening meal. I think they sometimes forget about the young man's presence. While I am sitting next to him and he is eating quietly, we hear my mother's melodious voice, Bilkisu's laughter, and the recurrent tuneful sound of tea being poured into glasses from the teapot lifted high in the air.

The Wife from the Journey

"Wake up, lazybones, the sun is already high in the sky! If you want to come to the palm grove with me, you'd better hurry."

Still dazed and sleepy, I stare at Bilkisu without understanding what she is saying.

"To the palm grove?" I say.

She laughs. "Did you forget that today is threshing day for the barley? Hurry up, or we'll miss the Arous ceremony!"

She gives me some very sweet green tea and a bit of cake. I devour them while she braids my hair and adjusts my *malafa*, the rectangle of embroidered wool tied under the chin with laces that girls wear on their heads until marriage. She sniffs my neck and frowns.

"My honey bun, I think you sweated last night. We will first stop at the baths to freshen up."

"But what about Abdelkarim? Who will take care of him?"

"I already brought him his lunch. Don't worry, he'll survive without you for one day," she says playfully.

I blush and lower my head. I don't dare confess that I am afraid of missing him. But the Arous ceremony is such an interesting sight! And who knows how long I'll still be allowed to go down into the palm grove?

We have to ask my mother for permission and she is working at her loom in a shady corner of the rooftop, her colorful skeins of wool spread out around her.

"Madame Meriem," says Bilkisu respectfully. "We're going to the baths, then I'll take Malika to the palm grove."

My mother looks me over solemnly, from head to foot. "Malika is becoming a young woman," she says. "Isn't it unseemly for her to go out into the street, even under your supervision?"

My mother, like all the women of high birth in Ghadames, hasn't set foot outside the house since her marriage, except to go to the baths. And she always goes to the baths at night, or when the men are at the mosque, and always she is wrapped in a thick veil that makes it impossible to tell whether she is young or old.

"Oh, Mama, let me go see the Arous! One last time . . ."

My mother sighs. "Indeed I think this will be the last year for you," she says, trying to soften her verdict with one of those smiles that melt my heart.

I quickly bend down and kiss her hand before dashing down the stairs hot on Bilkisu's heels. Ladi joins our expedition to help us carry the brass pitchers, the large white cotton towels and the fiber gloves we use to rub our skin.

How dark our street is! You have to know it well or you would be frightened in this pitch-black passageway where you have to feel your way at times. Many of our city streets are almost entirely covered to retain the coolness of the mud walls. The only lighting is provided, every fifty paces, by openings onto the sky; they let in shafts of light but are very narrow so they don't clog up during sandstorms. At night, a few torches are put up at the crossroads with gazelle horn good-luck charms; like the pointy horns on our rooftops, they are said to drive away the evil eye and the spirits of darkness.

To reach the women's baths of our neighborhood, we go down a passageway that is even narrower than the others and shaped like an elbow. For about twenty paces, we really can't see a thing. Ladi walks in front of us because she takes this road every day. In Ghadames, the servants don't sleep in their masters' houses; they have their own housing near the city walls.

Upon entering the passageway, Ladi groans plaintively several times: it's a signal that warns a male passerby that a woman is approaching. Caution! The loud thud of a foot stamped firmly on the ground tells us a man is coming toward us. Ladi retreats hurriedly and makes us stand in a recess in the wall until the man has gone by.

Bilkisu suppresses a giggle. "I'll never get used to this peculiar custom," she says to me in a whisper.

I find it bizarre too. And unfair. Why should a woman retreat just because she is a woman, even if she has almost reached the end of the passageway? Once, I was bold enough to ask my father. He looked embarrassed.

"You see, our ancestors thought it best to avoid contact between men and women who are not of the same family. We are used to this arrangement. But, from what I've been told, in some countries the customs are very different. There are places where men must make way for the women, and even greet them by baring their heads in their presence."

My mother was deeply shocked and refused to believe this. Why, that's an upside-down world! she said. Bilkisu was very intrigued. Did this mean, she asked, that in those countries women are considered superior to men?

My father smiled. No, he did not think so. It was merely a different custom.

That day, for the first time, I had a passionate desire to travel. It had never occurred to me before then that there were people who lived differently from us, who ate differently, who wore different clothes, and whose houses were built differently from ours. In the evening, lying on the rooftop where we sleep on summer nights, I saw the sky above me become infinite and sparkle with the constellations whose names and trajectories my father had taught me. Perhaps these other people call Deneb, Mizar and Altaïr by different names. Perhaps they don't share our belief that there is a big river of milk up there in the stars and that gazelles run along its riverbanks?

♦♦♦♦

We finally arrive at the baths. There is no signboard because the baths aren't meant for people who are not from our city. There is no door either, just a woman attendant who keeps men out.

You climb up three steps from the street and slip into a kind of hallway that has a row of six to eight cubicles separated by walls. Every bather sits at the edge of a little canal filled night and day with Ghadames springwater; the temperature of the water is always pleasant, winter and summer, and never has to be heated. There is a metal bar between the two walls for hanging clothes.

Today we are lucky; there are no other bathers and we can choose our place. I hate arriving last, and being at the end of the row, where you have to wait for the residues of soap and the remains of henna poultice with which the women coat their hair to be flushed away by the flow of water. This small annoyance occasionally gives rise to arguments. But this morning the only sound we hear is the lapping of the water from the movement of our feet in the canal, the water streaming out of the pitchers as we empty them over our naked bodies, and the song Bilkisu is humming in Hausa.

It feels good to have her scrub my shoulders and back, pumice the soles of my feet, and dig into my scalp with her fingers.

"A lovely garden soon to bloom," she whispers in our language.

"What garden are you talking about?"

"I'm talking about you, you're becoming a grown-up."

She has just poured a last pitcher of water over my head to rinse me off and looks at me very pensively as the clear water trickles down my shoulders, chest and legs. Suddenly I feel shy and I quickly slip on my tunic, which sticks to my moist back. Bilkisu gathers her braided hair into a bun at the nape of her neck; the hundreds of thin braids form two rounded mounds on each side of her forehead.

Jasim has her forehead, but he has our father's eyes.

"Bilkisu, how did you end up at our house?" I ask.

I know my voice sounds hostile, almost nasty, and I am ashamed again. Then I see her sunny smile. Bilkisu never gets angry. She just has a slightly amused way of looking at you that makes you feel naked, like a few minutes ago when she was rinsing me.

"I wasn't much older than you when I met your father," she says. "I was probably around thirteen, and at home it's like here, at thirteen a girl is certainly old enough to find a husband. My father wasn't rich, but he had a stall in the Kano market where he sold fine leather harnesses and saddlebags. He had been doing business with your father for years. No doubt he thought your father would treat me better than many of the men he knew. And he wasn't wrong."

"So my father married you before marrying my mother?"

I had never dared question my parents on how Bilkisu had become part of our family. There are two wives in many

Ghadames homes, the wife "from home" and the wife "from the journey," called that way because the master of the house has brought her back from afar. Often the wife from the journey comes from the south, like Bilkisu. Therefore many families in our city have two sets of descendants, one set with lighter skin and the other with darker skin, and the inheritance is divided equally between the two.

Bilkisu has already told me about Kano, which is several weeks away by foot, on the other side of the Sahara. It is as old a city as ours but much larger, and the walls are so thick that the enemies' spears break against them without making a dent. Jasim loves to hear her describe how, after the Ramadan fast, all the nobles of the region parade in front of the emir's palace on their magnificently harnessed horses. This makes my brother daydream: he sees himself at the head of the procession, wearing a tall gauze turban while the acrobats perform in the dust.

But Bilkisu has never told me how she met my father. She glances at Ladi, who is busy chatting with the attendant. Then she replies, lowering her voice:

"Your father was already married to your mother and did not hide the fact. Meriem, as you know, is his close cousin, promised to him from birth. Yet your father loved her instantly because she was so beautiful and well behaved, like an image he had always cherished in his heart. A perfect woman in the perfect city."

"A perfect woman in the perfect city." I echo her words

for they match the vision I have had of my mother since earliest childhood, and I despair of ever resembling her.

"Yes, he loved her and respected her," Bilkisu continues. "That's why it was painful for him when, having no children after over two years of marriage, his parents urged him to take another wife. Your father doesn't think much of this custom, though it is very widespread, here and in my city, and our religion allows it. Yet the Holy Book tries to discourage the practice by suggesting that a husband must treat his wives equally, which is extremely difficult.

"You can quantify bracelets and lengths of fabric, and give the same thing to each wife. But how can you quantify affection? Or measure tenderness? This habit of taking several wives suits most men too well for them to see its drawbacks. It engenders a lot of suffering and sometimes dreadful rivalries that endanger the fortune and unity of families."

"If he believes all this, why did he behave like the others?" I cry out, thinking bitterly of Jasim.

Oh, if only he had never been born!

I do not say this out loud, but Bilkisu understands. I often have the feeling that she is better at guessing my thoughts than my own mother.

"You would quarrel with Jasim even if he were Meriem's son and not mine," she says. "You both have lively temperaments, and he would still be a boy, determined to lord his male superiority over you. Nothing can be done about that. Aren't you glad to have me around? Your mother is an imposing lady," she adds tactfully. "I know she intimidates you and that it's hard for you to question her the way you question me."

That's true. I have nothing to say in response. Then Ladi starts to get impatient.

"Haven't you finished scrubbing yourselves?" she complains. "I have work to do. No one will clean the house if I don't. You'll get there after the Arous if you continue jabbering like that!"

She picks up the towels, the combs, the pitchers, and pushes us out the door. And there we part. Ladi goes to the left, while Bilkisu and I take an alleyway that leads to the gardens. We can already smell the sour aroma of fruit crushed in the dust, and the odor of droppings from the animals that press against the doors of the pens.

After the darkness, the abundant sun and vegetation come as a shock!

The gardens are surrounded by mud walls, but ornamented with openwork through which it's easy to see what is going on. In the morning, as long as it is not too hot, there is the coming and going of the women servants carrying big spheres of freshly cut grass for the animals, and of the men carrying spades on their shoulders. All you hear is the rustling of feet on the hardened earth and the twittering of birds high in the palm trees.

"Bah! What an odor!" says Bilkisu.

She has a keen sense of smell and quickly pulls me into a garden whose gate is open. Behind us, a man is carrying two large baskets filled with human fertilizer. True, it doesn't smell good. But the cesspits in the houses have to be emptied from time to time, so why not use the waste as fertilizer for the earth?

Bilkisu has told me how surprised she was to discover that in our houses the toilet is located at the top of the stairway, behind a brightly painted door. No bad odors come from it. The excrement falls into a pit that is located far below, at street level, and behind a wall, so as not to inconvenience the passersby. Once in a while, a hole is made in the masonry to remove the accumulated excrement, then quickly closed up again and forgotten about. It's a practical and useful system, like many things our ancestors invented.

"Look, beautiful lemons, Malika!"

Bilkisu likes lemon trees because they produce both blossoms and fruit. She finds this oddity of nature very amusing. She picks up a ripe lemon from the ground and bites into its skin with her teeth.

"Take it, it's a thirst quencher," she says.

"But this isn't our garden—"

"Bah! No one will begrudge us one lemon."

Emboldened by these words, we sit down at the foot of the lemon tree. The garden isn't very large, but it has all the essentials—a fig tree, a pomegranate tree, several date palms, tomato and onion plants, and grass for feeding the goats. In a corner, in the shade of the wall, there is an earthen jar with a wooden ladle attached to it; it contains cool water for refreshment.

"Do you want a drink?" Bilkisu asks.

I look at her reprovingly. She always looks cheerful and serene, like someone who has decided to be happy in the face of all opposition. Sometimes it annoys me.

"You did not really answer my question before," I say.

"What question?"

"How you came to Ghadames."

Bilkisu looks up at the sun, to gauge how much time we have left.

"Your father did not want a second wife," she says. "I begged him to take me with him. Otherwise, I knew my father would give me to another man, a Kano storekeeper who had already asked for my hand in marriage. That man frightened me. I was always uncomfortable when he looked at me."

I feel a twinge of sorrow. "And what about my father, didn't he look at you?"

She smiles. Her silver earrings dangle against her dark cheeks.

"Do you know that it was your father who wanted to teach me Arabic?" she says. "In our city, girls don't even attend Koranic school. They just recite their prayers, that's all. I was so proud to have a wooden board, a stylus and writing ink, like a boy. *Alif, bā, tā, thā* . . . I was very conscientious, and I could see that your father was pleased to see me write the letters of the alphabet correctly. He told me that Meriem had refused to learn to read and write. She believes that women will lose their powers if they pry and try to know the same things as men. Your father was sorry about that, yet he still talked about her with admiration. 'She is like a very pure metal,' he said, 'like a blade that strikes directly at my heart.'"

"She must have been sad when she saw you," I say.

"Oh, it was dreadful for both of us! I was expecting your brother, and after three unsuccessful years Meriem had given up all hope of ever having her own child. I thought she would break down before my eyes. But she gritted her teeth and welcomed me in her house. Your father was very attentive to her and spent a lot of time talking to her. She hardly spoke. She just listened. I stayed in my room and tried to make myself as inconspicuous as possible. It was my turn to be jealous. I thought of going back home, but the idea of the long trip in the desert with a child frightened me. We were like three wounded creatures who try not to move so as not to arouse pain. And then a miracle occurred: Meriem became pregnant as well. Another child was going to be born in our house! This changed everything. We prepared Jasim's arrival together, then yours. It was like an ongoing celebration.

"Now you understand," Bilkisu adds with a tender smile, "why you are as dear to my heart as any daughter of mine would be."

Suddenly, I respond with the gesture I usually reserve

for my mother: I kiss Bilkisu's hand. She jumps up as though I had burned her.

"The husband will already be wearing his red turban if we continue dallying like this!" she says.

I suddenly remember my mother's words. This will be my last Arous, the last one I will be allowed to attend. Afterward I will be confined to the rooftops, like the other women, and never come back down again.

So I open my eyes wide because I don't want to miss anything: the streaked shadow of the palm trees and the pale green of the apricot trees; the flight of the birds as they squabble in the branches; the footprint on the earth of an embankment, toes spread wide apart . . .

We come out on the threshing floor, which is always located in full sunlight and exposed to the most favorable winds. When it is time to winnow the grains, the wind does half the work. Barley matures earlier than wheat. The swathes have been lying in a dry spot for days, protected from the birds by palm tree branches and mats of esparto grass.

I see many people this morning around the threshing floor: women servants; slaves tending the gardens; slave masters accompanied by their children who are bubbling with excitement on this eventful day. Even my uncle is here and, next to him, Jasim, looking his conceited self in his sky blue gandourah carefully chosen to show his dark skin to advantage. Of course, on seeing me, all he can do is stick out his tongue! I would gladly stick mine out in response, except Bilkisu pushes me in the direction of the women before I have time.

Facing east, toward Islam's holy places, the laborers have started threshing the sheaves that are arranged in a circle. Each one is holding a *kerna*, the wide, hard base of a palm tree branch, and is beating the stalks to separate the grain. Their clothes are soon covered with straw debris, sweat runs down their temples, and their backs are soaked. Every once in a while, they drink from the jug that one of us hands them. Their work is sacred to everyone here. We reserve wheat semolina for pastries and holiday dishes, but we eat *bazina*, the thick porridge of barley flour, every day. It's perfect for filling hungry stomachs.

Finally, the great moment has arrived. The grains are gathered into a round heap and covered again with a mat. An elderly man traces Solomon's seal in the dust with his finger so as to protect the precious harvest from evil spirits.

"Youyouyouyouououou!"

The sound of ululation arises from the women's throats, a singsong wail that makes men shiver when they hear it. I would like to join in but my voice isn't strong enough yet and I am afraid of making a fool of myself in front of my brother. In the midst of the wailing, two women carry in a kind of doll they have made with bound palm twigs. This is Earth's husband, the Arous, and he will watch over the grain, wearing a fine red cloth turban.

The women's wailing grows louder for they must attract

the *baraka* on him, the benediction from heaven. Their call courses through me, from head to foot, and now I start wailing too, eyes shut, my throat vibrating almost painfully, as if my voice had to chart a new pathway through my body. I feel as though I am suddenly exposing myself fully.

Bilkisu takes me by the shoulders and kisses me.

"Bravo, you have the voice of a grown woman. It will soon be time to fill the bride's pitcher for you, from which you'll drink after your wedding night."

But the thought of a groom makes me dreadfully embarrassed and I bury my face in the folds of her veil.

When we return, I notice the look my mother and Bilkisu exchange when Bilkisu tells her about my vocal feats during the Arous ceremony. This means the end for me: from now on, like them, I'll have to be satisfied with the palm grove on the horizon and hearing the stories my father and brother bring back from their travels.

My mother does not say anything. But she spends a long time combing my hair and then, to see how it will look, she adorns my forehead with a heavy diadem of several rows of gold coins, the work of goldsmiths in faraway Timbuktu, which all the women in Ghadames wear at their marriage. She also lends me her favorite earrings. Then she leads me to the imbedded mirror above the door to the stairway.

I do not recognize myself. A strange girl peers at me from the clouded depths of the mirror, a girl whose eyes are ringed with bluish kohl, whose forehead is laden with gold, and who wears coral drops that quiver against her cheeks.

"See how lovely you are," my mother whispers.

She gently wipes a shiny teardrop from my cheek with the tip of her finger.

"Mama," I ask in a timid voice, "don't you miss going for walks in the palm grove? Aren't you tired of the red garden painted on the walls of the house?"

I see her smile slowly in the mirror, her eyes on my reflected image.

"No. For me, the red garden is more beautiful than the real one."

The Arabic Lessons

life is taking its course, with its countless household tasks—weaving, cooking, cleaning—and its little distractions. The wounded man is recovering his strength and I am spending more and more time in the pantry with him. Often he seems to forget that I am just a girl and he speaks to me as though I were a sensible grown-up worthy of interest. On these occasions I think of my father and wonder if he would like Abdelkarim.

Then I remember that my father is never ever supposed to find out that we have given shelter to a man in his absence.

One evening when I bring Abdelkarim his dinner, my mother starts singing and accompanying herself on the oud, the lute my father brought her from Tripoli.

> My heart feels crushed like a pomegranate
> My heart is trembling like a reed,
> My heart is green like new grass . . .

She interrupts herself, leaving the poem unfinished. The young man waits, but the next part never comes. The last rays of the sun shine through the half-open skylight and shed a golden light on his face.

"That's a beautiful song," he says regretfully.

"It's the 'Song of the Husband's Return.' Don't you know it?"

"I haven't been married. No one has sung it for me."

He falls silent for a moment. The sun must have descended below the rooftops, for everything darkens. Then, in an undertone, in a deep, low voice that isn't his usual timbre, he declaims in Arabic:

> I am seeking a refuge
> with the lord of the nascent dawn,
> Against the evil of the dark night
> when it descends on us,
> And against the evil of the women who
> blow on the knots,
> And the evil of the envious man who
> spreads envy.

"That's very beautiful," I say. "But I do not understand everything. I don't know Arabic very well."

"It's the sura of the nascent dawn, a chapter of the Koran. Don't you know the Koran?"

"A bit," I answer. "I don't know how to read." I feel I should explain. "I'd like to learn, but my mother says that women shouldn't know the same things as men, for men and women belong to two different worlds that hardly ever meet, like the sun and the moon."

"Oh, is that what your mother says? Yet the Koran is for everyone. It's the word of God," Abdelkarim says.

"Tell me, what does that mean, 'the women who blow on the knots'?" I ask.

"I think it's a reference to evil women who cast spells."

I shudder, thinking of Aïshatou. Is she one of those evil women? I pick up the empty dish at my feet. It is now almost impossible to see anything in the little room.

"Thank you for taking care of me, Malika. You're very kind, you know."

I look at him. I can make out his bright smile in the dark. For the first time, he no longer seems angry.

The following day, Aïshatou stops by to see him. To ward off any suspicions from our neighbors, with their dreaded eagle eyes, the tall black woman has come to read my mother's fortune in her coffee cup. Healer, witch, seer, midwife, she has the reputation of being all these things; and because of her varied talents, there are many reasons why she is in demand on the rooftops. For one woman, she'll predict whether she'll have a girl or a boy; for another, she'll prescribe a potion to reawaken the love of her apathetic husband. She can console a woman who has lost a very young child; help put a new mother back on her feet or increase her flow of milk. She knows all about bodily sufferings, and even more about those of the mind.

The reason all the women trust Aïshatou is because of her discretion. She never betrays a secret. She has buried many sorrows, and occasional passions as well, in the folds of her large black dress—between the worn leather pouches where she keeps her talismans and her medicinal powders.

My mother has prepared the coffee with great care. She has ground it very fine and mixed in some sugar, letting it boil very briefly in a brass pot with a long handle. Then you have to wait for the black foam to settle, pour the burning hot beverage into tiny cups, and add a drop of cold water to make the dregs sink to the bottom faster. Coffee should be savored with your eyes shut, so that its subtle perfume spreads in your mouth and rises up to your nostrils.

I'll only be allowed to taste a tiny bit. Coffee is a luxury for us; it comes from very far away, from the mountains of Yemen and Arabia. Part of our pleasure in drinking it derives from the long journey the caravans must make to bring it here. They cross landscapes so different from ours, and bivouac for weeks under the stars, the men sleeping on top of the sand-covered embers of the campfire to protect themselves against the cold desert nights. All these aspects of the journey are contained in those few black drops.

Aïshatou bends down and looks into my mother's empty cup. She turns it slowly between her fingers, taking care not to move the muddy black deposits on the bottom. This is because the barely visible mountains, the minuscule valleys, and the miniature rivers shimmering in the coffee dregs are all signs that foretell the future.

Aïshatou sets the cup down.

"There, you see," she whispers to my mother, who is now bending down too. "The stranger . . . your daughter . . . the jinn . . . your husband . . ." I can only catch bits and pieces of what she says. My mother's eyelids are half-closed. And what if all this were a lullaby, or like a nursery rhyme for children? Aïshatou stands up finally, makes sure no one is watching her from the surrounding rooftops, and steps calmly into the pantry signaling for me to follow.

The wounded man gazes at her with a worried look while she expertly removes his bandage and feels his pulse.

"The wound is healing well," Aïshatou says. "But you still need a few days' rest."

Abdelkarim sighs. "I am beginning to feel cramped, locked up in this cupboard like a goat in a pen," he complains.

"But it's your only hope of escaping your pursuers. Be patient. Within ten days, we will get you safely out of this house and out of the city."

"I don't want to leave this city," Abdelkarim says sullenly. "I've been given an important mission that must be successfully completed!"

"Haven't you ever heard the proverb, 'No man is a prophet in his own country'? Words of wisdom. Someone else will come to Ghadames to preach for the brotherhood that sent you. I have soothsaying powers, and that's what I read in the coffee dregs."

Abdelkarim sniffs contemptuously.

"I am not like you and your sort," he says. "You think you can see the future in the bottom of a coffee cup. Perhaps those predictions apply to women and their small, narrow world. God owns our destiny, but he leaves men free to shape it. He is the master of the future, but he also gives us the strength to spell out our own. Contrary to what you think, we are not his puppets."

Aïshatou looks down on him scornfully from her great height.

"No doubt you are right," she says. "But are women free? You'll soon have the opportunity to learn about their small, narrow world. Tomorrow, the women's market will take place on this and the neighbor's rooftop. The Ghadames houses take turns welcoming the market. We won't change what was planned, because we don't want anyone to think that Meriem has something to hide."

"But the women might see me!" Abdelkarim exclaims, suddenly alarmed.

"We will lock the door," Aïshatou announces with an ironic smile. "That way you will be condemned to hear us. That's a privilege very few men will ever have."

The women's market is one of the most entertaining daily events in Ghadames. It takes place on the rooftops in the morning, before it gets too hot. It's a treat for little children. They are fastened to their mothers' backs or skirts and stare at everything wide-eyed as their mothers move around the stalls—really just mats spread out on the ground.

The brouhaha is unbelievable, each saleswoman trying to attract attention to her merchandise, and every one exchanging the most varied news in a loud voice. I feel like laughing at the thought that this morning, Abdelkarim, hidden in the pantry, can hear what they are saying. At times, I even blush . . .

"Here are earrings shaped like crescent moons. Who will have them? Come and look at this beautiful coral necklace! Look at the color! Drops of dawn from the bottom of the sea. If only you knew what the sea is like, you desert girls."

"Soap made with the best olive oil, from Gharyān, the mountains in the north! Soap that will make your skin nice and soft, ladies!"

"Do you know that my cousin Nejma had a baby last night?"

"I heard the cries announcing a birth early this morning, but I was too far away to understand the message. Girl or boy?"

"A fourth girl. May God protect her from her husband's wrath! But Aïshatou predicted that her next child would be a boy. Let's hope she's not just saying that to cheer her up."

"Taste these lovely dried figs. They're like honey."

"Alas, you know, I don't have very much money since

my husband died, nor do I have anything to give you in exchange."

"It doesn't matter. Take half of them for your children, you'll pay me when you can. Who knows what the future will bring?"

"Fatima! Why don't you keep an eye on your son? He just spilled a whole box of kohl, the little devil!"

"Doesn't anyone want to buy this fresh milk before it turns sour? I milked the goat myself at dawn."

"Meriem, your daughter is becoming very pretty. It looks like her breasts are growing. And what eyes! Soon it will be time to plan her wedding, won't it? I have a nephew who is looking for a wife, I'll speak to him discreetly."

"Don't be in such a rush. She still has to mature—"

"Like a lovely little fig on the branch—ha, ha!"

"Here, Zohr, take this portion of flour, I am in debt to you for the favor you did me the last time."

"What favor?"

"You don't remember? I know times are hard when one is disowned and one must return to one's parents' house. You're still young, you'll find another husband, God willing!"

Each woman gives whatever she can today, generously and taking care not to humiliate, but also as a precaution. Who knows if she herself won't experience poverty tomorrow? Who knows what tragedies life has in store for her? Ever since I was little, I've seen our women stock up on solidarity, like ants that tirelessly carry on their backs what they'll need to survive the bad season.

Protecting themselves from misfortune, that is their prime concern. Our women's bodies are covered with tattoos, guarding them like an armor against mysterious enemies. At the market, I watch them closely and with curiosity. Knowing that no men are looking at them, they throw their veils back so that they can be freer in their movements; they uncover their arms, necks and ankles, adorned with geometrically shaped bluish marks. They have other marks, hidden in secret places and visible only at the baths. Women's bodies are like books; you have to know how to decipher them.

For the first time I dare to question my mother.

"Mama, what's that broken line you all have above the ankle?"

My mother hesitates. But she must have decided that now I am old enough to know.

"We call it the sickle. It's meant to give us many children and good harvests."

"And the little strokes on a line?" I press.

"The comb, because women must take good care of their hair. This one, which looks similar but has a kind of handle underneath it, is the comb for weaving, because every self-respecting woman knows the art of weaving."

She explains the complicated motifs that crisscross on the back of her hands, from the top of her wrists to her nails: the saber, the saw, the reed leaves. But I get mixed up very quickly. What I am most interested in are the animals. Their shapes are so simplified that I couldn't possibly identify them if Mama did not show them to me, whispering as though the designs themselves are actually dangerous.

"Look, here's the snake that brings fertility, the scorpion that bites evildoers. And those four intersecting straight lines there are the paws of the tarantula, a spider that will inflict a painful bite on our rivals."

Examining these tattoos on smooth skin or skin wrinkled with age—tattoos whose meanings have long been concealed from me—makes me pensive. I no longer know what to think. So women can be kind and help one another. But they can also be the worst enemies, jealous rivals in secret, with a wish to harm one another. Do they sometimes ask Aïshatou for potions to take revenge? For poisons that kill?

When all the women are gone, we go to free Abdelkarim, who is still locked up in the pantry. Bilkisu opens the door. Abdelkarim looks at us reproachfully and takes the cake I hand him without saying a word.

"Have you stopped speaking to us?" asks Bilkisu. "Why are you in such a foul mood?"

Since he doesn't deign to answer, Bilkisu shrugs and heads toward the door.

"Wait," he says. "Since I have to spend another nine days here, there is one thing that would amuse me."

"Your wish is our command," Bilkisu says ironically. "State your wish."

"I'd like to teach Malika how to read. Would her father take offense?"

Bilkisu seems surprised. She drops her ironic tone and becomes very serious.

"No, he wouldn't. He wanted his daughter to learn Arabic, and he taught it to me. Meriem is the one you have to persuade."

"Then I would like to talk to her about it."

As soon as Bilkisu has turned on her heels to warn my mother, I question Abdelkarim anxiously. I want to be sure I understood correctly. Does he really want to give me lessons—me, even though I am just a girl?

For the first time today, he allows himself to smile. He is handsome when he smiles.

"Girls deserve to be taught just as much as boys. It's because they aren't taught anything that they wallow in all that foolish nonsense, all that magic stuff and coffee dregs."

My mother comes in, tightly wrapped in an austere veil baring only her face. She stops at the threshold, as though afraid of something, then gestures to me to sit farther off on the rooftop, but facing the cupboard door, which remains open. I understand that she wants a witness to this meeting, that she needs eyes steadily on her, to testify nothing improper has happened between the two of them.

Abdelkarim has backed into the room as much as possible. He is sitting under one of the small skylights. An oblique ray of afternoon sunlight is shining down from it. If my mother occupies the place he has made for her, her face will be lit up while his features will blend into the darkness. She hesitates, but finally steps forward.

I now see both of them in profile. My mother is staring at him with no fear or shame, her eyes wide open. I am trembling, for I know what my mother's gaze is like—a burning black ray of light beamed from under eyebrows that are almost joined together. I predict that he—not she—will lower his eyes.

I can't hear what Abdelkarim is saying, but now and again he turns his face my way. My mother doesn't move. She looks at him steadily. From time to time, he tilts his head while she is speaking. Her voice is very gentle and she never speaks for long. Her gaze is sufficiently eloquent. I watch their duel from a distance but I can't guess who the winner will be.

Oh, if only he could convince her! But she is so strong, so inflexible. I have a powerful urge to finally see her weak and defeated; I wish she were an ordinary woman made of clay instead of pure metal. I immediately blame myself for this sacrilegious thought. If she knew, she wouldn't love me anymore. I bury this desire deep within me and keep it well hidden. In the end, I don't dare breathe or even think. I clench my teeth for fear that if my breath escapes from my lips, it might tilt the scales against me.

Abdelkarim has still not lowered his eyes. Suddenly, from the way my mother bows her neck slightly, and draws in her shoulders, I know she has surrendered and acquiesced. She opens the palms of her hands, looks at them pensively, and raises them toward the sky in acceptance of God's will. My heart is filled with joy, almost painfully so. He has won.

That night, in the little room above the stairway, I find it hard to fall asleep. I feel my father's books around me, like a living presence pursuing me even in my dreams.

The following day, as soon as my brother has left for our uncle's store, I start studying the alphabet with Abdelkarim. Early in the morning it is still cool in the pantry, and that first lesson will always be associated in my mind with the smell of honey and the dust of dry figs—figs strung up on cords and piled up in a large straw basket at the far end of the room.

Abdelkarim is surprised that I brought a board and stylus with me. I explain how I won them in my race with Jasim on the rooftops. As I tell him about it, I experience everything all over again: the vertigo paralyzing my legs, the joy of daring to challenge my brother, and the satisfaction of triumphing over fear.

He looks at me, even more surprised. "You must truly have wanted to learn to read and write, risking your life like that," he says.

"At the time, I did not even think about it," I answer. "I just wanted to annoy Jasim. He had made me mad."

"This means you'll be a good student," Abdelkarim says,

smiling. "People who remain indifferent or too submissive never learn much. Whatever they're taught is like water off a duck's back. Their brains never really absorb anything. Sometimes it's good to get mad."

As Abdelkarim says this, he can't help glancing at my mother, who is sitting by her loom, impassive. They have agreed that she will be present at each lesson, sitting not too far away, but not too close either, so as not to disturb us. She looks our way very infrequently, but we hear the dry, reassuring sound of the curved reed she uses to space the warp yarns evenly.

First my teacher prepares the ink, mixing black powder and water in a glass flask. Then he carefully writes out the twenty-eight Arabic letters from right to left, pronouncing each one of them clearly and making me repeat them. The letters have strange shapes. Some resemble reeds bending in the wind; others, birds with flexible necks and folded wings; still others, gondolas, those flat, lightweight, cradle-like boats I once saw when my father took me to a small lake a half-day's walk from Ghadames. Some of the letters are very easy; one line is enough. Others require such complicated squiggles that I would be afraid of getting muddled recopying them.

But on that first day, Abdelkarim teaches me only one word: *bâ-boun*, the door, until I can write it perfectly. He is pleased with me; his eyes are twinkling.

"That's enough for today," he says, propping the board, ink and stylus against the wall.

I feel so happy that I start singing as I go down the stairway. Ladi, who is in the large room busily polishing our brass vases, looks up with a mocking air.

"No one thought of teaching me how to read," she says.

"Ladi, once I've learned, I'll teach you."

"That's what you say now, because you're happy, but you'll always have better things to do than to bother about me."

She is right. I am already obsessed with just one thing—looking at my father's books. He doesn't have very many, only about four or five, but he truly values them. "They allow me to see other things," he always says when I ask him what he finds in these yellowed pages.

I wonder if I will find things in them that I never saw before. I touch their bindings, their rounded backs, the faded gold lettering stamped on dark leather, but I don't dare open them. They have a distinctive smell that I've always liked, a smell of dusty leather and cooled sand that reminds me of my father's smell. Isn't that letter on the cover a *bâ*, and that other one a *boun*? I remember Bilkisu going over my brother's lessons with him, and my despair at not being able to understand a thing.

I also remember feeling that a door was forever closed within me. Perhaps now it is finally opening. . . .

The Cavalcade of Jinn

"Me, dress up as a woman? What about my dignity? It's out of the question, I'll never agree! I'd rather die."

Abdelkarim has become livid. By contrast, the barely healed scar on his forehead looks darker. Bilkisu and I exchange glances in dismay.

As always when she is in Abdelkarim's presence, my mother stands back, her profile impassive. Not Bilkisu. I see her nostrils quiver and the upturned corner of her mouth. I know she is dying to make a caustic remark in reply. But it would be dangerous. It is wiser to try to convince the obstinate young man while there is still time.

"But there's really no other solution," she pleads, containing her anger. "You can't stay here any longer. We were told by a traveler that Mahmud's caravan would be returning within two or three days. Have you thought of the consequences for us, who saved your life? Believe me, you won't lose your dignity just from covering your head with a woman's veil for a few hours."

It was Aïshatou's idea and it was probably mixed with a bit of malice. The plan was to make the fugitive leave the city during one of the night ceremonies from which men are excluded. These are ceremonies that occasionaly take place in the palm grove. On those nights, no one is surprised to see female silhouettes sneak outside the city walls—certainly not the guardians posted at the city gates. Who would ever bother to count the women returning at daybreak from a festival celebrated since time immemorial far from the eyes of the indiscreet?

"And what if he refuses?" objected Bilkisu. I strained to follow their discussion, pressed against my mother's side. Their dark veils, turned down over their lowered foreheads, formed a dark little hiding place, muffling their whispered words.

"He'd better accept," mumbled Aïshatou. "If he doesn't . . ."

She fell silent, alerted by Bilkisu's frown. I felt my mother shudder, and I looked at Aïshatou's hands and the heavy bracelets clasped around her wrists.

If he doesn't? Not one of us completed the sentence out loud, but my stomach was tied in knots from fear.

They leave me with him. Though they do not say anything, I know they are counting on me to make him change his mind. But I can't speak at all. I am too choked up.

◆◆◆◆

When Abdelkarim first started giving me lessons, he did not foresee that we would progress so rapidly. We work in the morning, when it's still cool, and again in the afternoon, reviewing the morning lesson. Every day he is surprised at my resolve, and every day I am determined to forge ahead as I race toward a still invisible goal. When I reach it I will be saved. From what? All I know is I must keep racing ahead, which constantly reminds me of my footrace with Jasim. That evening, poised on the edge of the roof, I felt in less danger than now, when I am terrified of falling into a bottomless pit if I take just one step back . . .

Jasim often complained about his schoolmasters, who corrected students' mistakes by hitting them on their shaved heads with a stick. But Abdelkarim, with his great contempt for ignorant women, never gets annoyed when I forget to put in the accents, or when I mix up the forms of the letters at the beginning of a word with those that go in the middle or at the end. Oh, those letters that change completely with their position in a word, like dunes in the wind!

Once, he looked up from the writing board and smiled. "Before coming here, I saw myself inspiring crowds with the beauties of religion, and in my mind I saw crowds of men, only men," he said. "But God tests our pride. It could be that I was sent to this city to teach the alphabet to a girl. Your perseverance is a sign."

On another occasion, just once, he said to me, "You look like your mother."

Yet he never looks at her. Well, hardly ever. I know because I always watch him out of the corner of my eye when she is near us, sitting at her loom—or grinding barley grains with a millstone until her hands are completely covered with a feathery, white dust that forms light-colored circles on her black veil.

Today Abdelkarim remains silent for a long time. Standing against the door, I wait for him to make up his mind.

"So, you think I should leave the city too?" he asks.

"What other solution is there? It's a great stroke of luck that the ceremony is taking place," I answer. "That way you'll be able to leave without anyone noticing you. It will be better for us."

"Have you ever been to this women's festival?"

"Me? No. Until now, they never wanted to include me. All I know is, when they return, they always look happy. My father says it purges them of all their demons, and that men ought to find a way of doing the same!"

But soon something else worries him. "Those Tuaregs that Bilkisu mentioned, can they be trusted?" he asks.

I nod. "They are Iforhas. Their encampment is next to those tall stones that I am sure you know, stones so old that it is a mystery who put them there. Aïshatou sometimes goes there at daybreak and stretches out on the stones. She says they tell her secrets about the future. The Iforhas' blacksmiths have the same abilities as her. They know the language of the stones and formulas for curing people. And they respect Aïshatou as one of their own. If she asks them to take you to a safe place, they won't betray you."

He sighs. "When will we have to leave?"

"That depends on the moon. It could be tomorrow night."

"So this will be our last lesson."

With a heavy heart, I pick up the board propped against the wall and sit down next to him. We work nonstop, until the little room becomes dark and our eyes are so tired the lines blur. Then my teacher stands up and stretches his fingers. Mine are numb from so much writing. But we've gone through the entire alphabet.

"You've made enormous progress in a very short period of time. It's a shame we have to stop now. I hope you won't let your mind lie fallow."

I am reminded of a family garden in the palm grove, left abandoned by the two brothers who owned it, because they did not get along anymore. Dry grass covers the land, the dates disintegrate into dust, the lower branches of the fruit trees droop to the ground. Even the birds have stopped singing. Is that what my poor brain will look like soon?

But I don't dare tell him about my fears, or mention the pit that haunts my dreams and that I am terrified of falling into. I say the first thing that comes to mind, just so I can stay with him a bit longer:

"Abdelkarim, does your family own much land in the palm grove?"

"They used to, but now I don't know. I am not very interested in agriculture. Does your father own much land?"

I shake my head. "Just enough to give us some fruit. My father prefers to put his money into his business, with associates whom he trusts in Kano and Istanbul. He says trade brings in more money. And also . . ."

I feel embarrassed.

"And also?" Abdelkarim prompts.

"My father doesn't like the idea of owning slaves. Here, if you own a lot of land, you have to have slaves, for farming, for repairing the irrigation ditches which bring the springwater into the gardens, for picking up fertilizer, for performing all those tasks that the people of Ghadames consider beneath their dignity."

Abdelkarim seems surprised. "So your father doesn't own slaves, unlike all the great families here?"

"No, he doesn't. Even my mother couldn't make him change his mind." I feel I should explain. "He has often told us how he resolved never to own slaves during his first trip across the Sahara with his uncle. They found two skeletons at the edge of the road, whitened by the sun, two women whose hands were tied with rope. You could still see their earrings and their dresses in tatters. They must have been very young when they died because their teeth were in perfect condition, absolutely intact.

"My father was horrified. As a child he had become accustomed to seeing slaves in the streets and the gardens of Ghadames. But now, for the first time, he realized what it was like to be torn away from one's family, thrown on the roads, and taken to unknown lands with no hope of returning. He vowed to himself never to be the cause of such misfortune and he has kept his word. He has never bought or sold a human being."

Abdelkarim looks at me pensively. "You admire your father a lot."

"Oh, yes! He has ideas that my uncles don't have. He is always interested in new things. And he talks to me as though I were a grown-up."

Abdelkarim smiles. "But you'll soon be a grown-up." Then his gaze darkens. "I wish I could meet your father. It's a pity I have to leave."

The following day, they give me the task of bringing Abdelkarim a large, neatly folded piece of black cloth.

"This is an armor that will protect you from your enemies," I say solemnly.

Abdelkarim looks at me, frowning. Is he already angry? Bilkisu lectured me at length: "Whatever you do, don't use the word *veil*. Avoid it like the plague! He must not feel insulted or think that you're making fun of him!" Bilkisu repeated this advice over and over again. I am doing my best. My jaws are aching from suppressing any semblance of a smile.

But to my astonishment, in the space of a night he has gotten used to an idea that infuriated him a day ago, and this morning he is as gentle as a lamb.

"You'll have to help me," he says simply.

◆◆◆◆

Today is a special day for me too, because my mother gave me my first young girl's veil, a dark blue fabric that I've draped over my *malafa*. I show Abdelkarim how to keep the veil drawn shut, with the edge wedged between one's teeth, and how to walk so as to outwit our vigilant city guards. For, as everyone knows, men and women walk differently.

"Look, men step putting their heels down first, in manly, self-confident fashion, whereas women put their toes down first, timidly, in a way that befits an inferior creature. That's how we're taught to walk by our mothers when we're very little, and heaven help us if we forget it!"

Abdelkarim stares at me, wide-eyed. "Do you mean to say that women have to learn to walk like women, and that if their mothers did not correct them, they would tread on the ground as men do?"

Now, it's my turn to be troubled. This had never occurred to me.

But I am even more embarrassed at suddenly being the teacher, and at Abdelkarim being the student, a strange student with a beard and mustache. I bite my lip painfully several times so as not to burst out laughing. We certainly make an odd couple, tangled up in our veils, taking cautious, little steps as though the room were carpeted with fragile eggs or feathers. I only hope the guards will not be looking our way when we go through the city gate.

Silence now. The time has come to weave our way through the streets next to my mother and Bilkisu, both as snugly wrapped as we are. Whispering figures file ahead of us and we are joined by more and more of them, as the discreet but repetitive scraping of dozens—no, hundreds—of leather soles tread on the hardened mud—toes first!

Each time a door opens, we see the oil lamp in the cavity of the entryway conforming to the immutable code: the master is at home. He may be home, but his wife and the women next door are all making their way through the dark torchlit alleyways. This female procession in a flickering half-light is a rather bizarre sight.

We cross the small Mulberry Square, where the slave market is located. I have always found the dark arcades sinister, as if tragedy were permanently ingrained in the walls in spite of the purifying layers of whitewash regularly applied to them.

The procession must then cross Gâddous Square. This is the name we give to the iron cup that is held by a child seated in a cement niche. Under the niche is a *seguia*, one of the narrow ditches that brings water to the palm grove. For centuries this is the way we have been measuring the outflow of our spring so that we can divide it equitably.

Day and night the child fills the cup with water and hangs it above the ditch. From a small hole at the bottom of the cup, the water slowly empties out. Each time the cup is filled, the child ties a knot in a long palm-leaf filament. The *Amine el Mâ*, the water controller appointed by the city residents, must be able to check the outflow at any given moment. So the cup serves as the measuring unit for irrigation. This is accomplished by blocking the openings of the *seguias* with earth, or unblocking them, depending on the time and the size of the gardens.

Filling and tying, day and night. The children take turns in the niche but they all end up looking the same, with sad, prematurely aged faces, worn out by the monotonous work. Whenever I see clear, fresh water flowing through the *seguias* in the palm grove, I think of the child sitting in the Gâddous niche.

When we reach the city walls, on the eastern side, we find that the guards posted under the archway have left the palm-trunk gate open. No greetings are exchanged. These men don't even seem to see us. Tonight the rules governing our lives are mysteriously suspended. Tonight the women of Ghadames belong to another world that will vanish with the first glimmer of dawn.

The moon, already high in the sky, can be seen through the branches of the palm grove, round and white, like a basin of curdled milk.

Zam-ʐam! Tap-tapa! Zam-ʐam!

We hear the throbbing of the *bendirs* and *derbukas* being struck by the women musicians with their callused palms.

Zam-ʐam! Tap-tapa! Zam-ʐam!

We finally stop near the half-crumbled ruins. I have never been in this faraway corner of the palm grove and am surprised to see a kind of vessel covered with a tall earthen vault. The musicians are seated all around it, beating on the resonant skins of the drums.

"This is the other spring, our spring," whispers my mother, taking me firmly by the hand. "There has to be water for the jinn to visit human beings. Water always attracts them."

"Mama, aren't you afraid of the jinn?"

"I am afraid of them when I am alone. Tonight, everything is different."

A dozen women are undressing hurriedly. They leave their clothes hanging on the trunk of a tilted palm tree at the edge of the vessel and wade into the water up to their waists, twisting their damp hair. Two oil lamps project enormous, monstrous shadows under the vault. I squeeze my mother's hand very tightly, and press my face against the side of her body. But she raises my head.

"You have no reason to be frightened," she says gently.

Some other women start dancing and soon they are nearly all swaying at the shoulders and hips, their necks very straight and their heads held high, almost motionless. The musicians play with increasing vigor. A very powerful music is required to summon the jinn and to make the dancers gyrate until they collapse, exhausted. There are lamps placed in a circle and scented resin burning on small burners.

Zam-zam!

The musicians are old. Gold coins from Timbuktu shine

on their black foreheads. They laugh as they strike the skin tambourines faster and faster, staining them with droplets of sweat. It is impossible to resist this music. It flows into the shoulders, chest and legs, making the whole body vibrate with a long, painful trembling. I join the dance, submerged, jostled, swept up by an invisible force.

Zam-zam! Tap-tapa! Zam-zam!

Then some women around me start saying mad, incomprehensible things in loud voices. Who are they talking about? One invokes a king out loud. Another, the red minister, but who is this minister? Yet another falls onto the ground, yelling "He slapped me!" I open my eyes wide, but I don't see anyone. The woman grasps her cheek and moans, then is immediately surrounded by a buzzing wave of women who console her and sweep her far away from me.

I want to be safely near my mother, whom I see sitting at Aïshatou's feet with other women from noble families. Aïshatou is enthroned in their midst, like a king at court, and they call her "Princess." How strange. The world seems upside down.

Aïshatou looks at me with her yellowish gaze, and her lips smile slowly.

"Meriem," she says finally, "do you want to show your daughter how women straddle the jinn, and how the jinn take them farther than any desert track?"

A few women grab me and pet my body laughingly, encouraging me with their voices and gestures. Suddenly, I can't stand having them touch me. And I have a headache, a dreadful headache! I leap up and run away, with just enough time to see Aïshatou put her large black hand on my mother's arm to stop her from following me.

I don't know how I managed to break through the circle. My head feels both empty and clouded, as though I had slept in air saturated with sweat and powerful perfumes.

Outside, the night is chilly. The moon, veiled with smoky mist, is very low on the horizon and barely visible through the palm trees. My mind is a bit clearer now. I walk toward the shepherd's hut where we hid Abdelkarim when we arrived.

He is still there, shivering, waiting for dawn, wrapped in his veil that is too thin for the cold desert nights.

"Is that you, Malika?" he asks, worried. "When will they be coming?"

"When the ceremony is over," I say. "I'll keep you company. That should make time go faster."

I crouch outside, near the entrance. I am suddenly aware of being alone with him, but I know nothing can really happen to me tonight. It is as though I had been given some of the strength that aroused the women when they danced and this has buttressed my shoulders. I look up at the sky. Tanit . . . Wasn't she the moon goddess in very ancient times? That little silver moon we wear as pendants on bracelets. And the enormous one that appears periodically in the night sky only to dissolve when the voices of the muezzins resound from the minarets.

"It's so dark," says Abdelkarim in a low voice. "It's a good thing you came. I was beginning to feel frightened."

"Frightened of what?"

"Of the night. Of the desert. Once—"

He breaks off with a sudden coughing fit. Then he catches his breath. "I was around five or six. I had gone with my father by camel about an hour away from here, near those ruins called Ras el Ghoul, the hill of ghosts. I am sure you've heard of it. He wanted to see a shepherd who was looking after some of his livestock. In those days there was still a well under the ruins, a trickle of water that flowed to the end of a narrow, crumbling gully. The shepherd knew how to find it. It provided enough water for his own needs, and grazing grass for the baby camels.

"I walked away while he and my father were talking. I had started going around the hill, just a rocky peak, but it seemed like a long distance for a small child. Suddenly the sky turned red. In a few minutes, everything was engulfed in a violent sandstorm. Like all desert children I had been told repeatedly what to do if caught in one of those storms."

"Sit down immediately, cover your head, and wait," I recite without a moment's thought. "We're taught this when we're very small! Above all, don't walk, or no one will find you."

"Yes, I'd been told this," says Abdelkarim again, sadly. "But I must have forgotten. It was the first time I was in danger in the desert. I had always lived safely inside the city walls. Up ahead I thought I saw the ridge of the ruins at the top of the peak. I ran and called for my father. Then I thought I could see the hump of a camel in the swirls of sand, and I ran even faster, convinced I would soon reach my father or his shepherd. It took me quite a while to realize I had gone astray and was completely lost.

"Only then did I sit down, bury my head between my arms, and cover my mouth with a flap of my tunic. Night fell, and though the wind died down a bit, you really couldn't see anything! What a night! I felt the air enveloping me with its thousand invisible hands, and I thought I might be carried away forever by the genies of the desert. It was the shepherd who found me, in the morning."

"And your father?" I ask.

His voice breaks. "He must have gone very far looking for me. Two weeks later, travelers journeying down the bed of a dried out wadi discovered his body. He is buried there, under a heap of stones."

My hands suddenly turn so cold that I raise them to my lips.

"Ever since then," whispers Abdelkarim, "I can't spend a night without praying. I really only start breathing normally at dawn, with the first cry of the muezzin."

Then, very slowly, Abdelkarim starts chanting the sura he had recited for me on the rooftop.

> I am seeking a refuge
> with the lord of the nascent dawn,

Against the evil of the dark night

when it descends on us . . .

"I remember that sura. That's the one that led to your teaching me the alphabet."

"There are several sorts of darkness in us," says Abdelkarim. "Ignorance is one."

"I know. I want to continue learning. I don't want my brain to lie fallow again."

For the first time that night, I see him smile.

"All the better. But I wasn't thinking about your ignorance, but about my own. I learned several things while I was hidden on your rooftop. For example, that the world of women is not as stupid as I thought."

I laugh. "Thank you. You're too kind. So, we've both learned something."

"Yes, we've both learned something. Please tell your mother and Bilkisu, since I can't tell them myself. I know I won't see them again."

Meanwhile, the sky has gradually turned pink and the last stars are fading. In the east, behind the dark row of trees, a strip of light is growing wider. The noise of footsteps puts us on the alert. It is Ladi guiding a tall, thin man down the path. He is veiled in black, carrying one of those long, leather bags with multicolored fringes that the Tuaregs fasten on their saddles.

Everything goes very quickly. After some brief greetings, I see Abdelkarim wrap a thin, dark cloth around his hair, like a crown, carefully hiding his mouth. With this mask, he takes on the impenetrable look of a desert nomad. When he stands straight, draped in a large blue gandourah with pleats at the shoulder, he looks taller than usual and I think I never would have recognized him in a crowd.

"Farewell," he says, leaning toward me. "If I can, I will give you news."

And in a minute he is gone.

The Return

It always starts with a cry, so far away that it blends with the other sounds in the city. Our hearts beat fast and we lower our heads for fear of being wrong. We can never be sure when we hear the first cry.

Then it comes closer, bouncing from rooftop to rooftop, carried and amplified by the mouths of a hundred women:

"He has returned . . ."

"Lord Mahmud!"

"Safe and sound from the desert . . ."

"Lord Mahmud!"

"His caravan is loaded with beautiful things . . ."

"Lord Mahmud . . ."

"Take out your jewels, Meriem and Bilkisu!"

That is how the wives in Ghadames learn about the arrival of the caravans; the news spreads across the rooftops throughout the city even before the travelers have had time to dismount. Soon they look up and see the city walls. In the last few days, they have endured fatigue, scorpions, vipers and sandstorms, so that they could once again hear the voices of the invisible women, the concert they give for every return.

At home, everyone wakes up. Jasim runs to Uncle's store and rushes down the alleyways to welcome his father, who is supervising the unloading of the camels. Ladi has brought out the most beautiful pillows and is carefully sweeping the stairway. My mother and Bilkisu open the little wooden chests in which they hide their jewelry.

It is as if they had been in mourning while my father was far away. Now they can again wear jewelry and look beautiful. In their earlobes they hang silver drops that dangle gently against their cheeks; they slip on bracelets and anklets with resonant names—*tahadidiène, khalkhal*—ornaments that punctuate their footsteps around the house.

Around their necks, they fasten necklaces made of fragrant grains, a blend of wood powder kneaded with rose petal, clove, nutmeg, scented water and ambergris. On their tunics, they pin a brooch in the shape of a scorpion, with a metal sting to protect them against misfortune and jealousy. Their smiles are full of secrets. As for me, I can't help wondering: doesn't each one, deep down in her heart, wish she were the only wife?

The morning light reflects off the mirrors, illuminating the large room ready to welcome my father. Above our heads, the rows of brass vases glow magnificently. Festive cakes, filled with pistachios and coated with honey, are in the pantry waiting to be served. Everything is all set.

Bilkisu starts singing the song of the return in her high-pitched voice:

My heart feels crushed like a pomegranate
My heart is trembling like a reed . . .

Yet it is my mother who plucks the strings of her oud and sings the last stanza:

The stonemason builds the houses
The blacksmith works on the locks
The carpenter adjusts the doors
And Mahmud is my lord!

Usually I hesitate to talk to my mother when I know she may get angry. But right now I am so furious that it gives me courage, as when I raced Jasim.

"Why do women sing of the doors and locks that prevent them from going out? Is that because they are actually pleased to be locked up?" I ask.

Mama looks at me, her eyes so dark under the black furrow of her eyebrows.

"No, they are not pleased," she says. "But with time you will learn that no person who loves, whether man or woman, is ever completely free."

I finally ask the question that has been tormenting me for three days. "Will you tell my father about what happened in his absence?" I say.

Mama hardly bats an eyelid, then shakes her head. "Not now. One day, I am sure, we'll find a way of telling him. I also know why you're worried. You're afraid of not learning to read anymore."

I lower my head, relieved she has guessed my thoughts.

"Don't worry, I won't go back on my promise. You'll learn, since it means so much to you! Your desire is so strong I can't go against it anymore. And then, Aïshatou told me it was time to accept certain changes."

On the rooftops, the ululation concert continues, an indication the travelers are now inside the city walls.

"They've crossed the Aïn el Fars gate!"

"He has stopped at the Gâddous fountain . . ."

"He is greeting the old men on Mulberry Square . . ."

Here he is at last! Preceded by a Jasim who is overexcited and prances up the stairway. Poor Jasim. He has been unhappy ever since he was expelled from the rooftop and his face has looked somber, like a lamp which has used up its oil supply. Now he is beaming with pride; he feels like the king of the world again.

"Look at the dagger my father brought me from his trip up north! Look at the horn handle, and how sharp the blade is," he tells me. "It isn't iron, it's steel, a very shiny, very hard metal. I bet you never saw this metal before!"

"And neither did you. I bet you never saw it before either!" I say, making my worst possible grimace.

But then I blush because my father has just appeared at the top of the stairs. He frowns.

"Is that the grumpy face with which you welcome your father?" he says. "Stop quarreling, at least when I am around."

Yet he's not really mad. Just tired. I watch him surreptitiously as he sits down on the cushions, takes off his turban, and massages his temples and eyelids with his fingertips. He has rings under his eyes, his features are drawn from the long journey, and there are more gray patches in his hair than before. I realize my father is not as young as I thought. Or else it's me who suddenly feels older.

Huffing, puffing, and grumbling, Ladi has brought a large basket up the stairs. My father never fails to bring back gifts for each one of us whenever he makes a trip. Ladi, first in line, inspects the fabric of two remnants of purple cloth with white stripes, in fashion in the north. She will use them to make herself a dress for the next wedding celebration, she says, peering at me out of the corner of her eye. My mother receives about thirty skeins of fine wool in warm colors, including a saffron yellow and a red the color of pepper, colors which will look beautiful in the rugs she works on so patiently.

"And what's that?" exclaims Jasim when he sees Papa extract a strange object from a bag. It is a metal lamp and on it, he places a big glass tube, which had been packed separately in a cocoon of rags.

He shows us how to fill the tank with a yellow liquid

and soak a thick braided wick in it that will burn slowly, shedding a rather strong light.

Most astonishing is the little key affixed to the neck of the lamp that you turn to lower or raise the light—an improvement that doesn't exist on our oil lamps, which, it must be said, do not produce much light.

Everyone goes into raptures, but my mother looks at it disapprovingly.

"It smells bad," she objects. "And where will we find this liquid you call kerosene? We don't have any here."

"That's just it," says my father, proud of his discovery. "I've ordered some from my associate. During my next trip to Tripoli, I plan to bring back a large quantity of liquid and many lamps to sell to the residents of Ghadames."

Jasim and I jump up and down enthusiastically. We are sure this lamp will sell well, especially during the Ramadan evenings when people like to stay up late.

"What better light than the sun can ever be found for human beings?" asks Mama, always suspicious.

Then, from a goatskin portfolio, my father takes out Bilkisu's surprise: a printed book, with illustrations showing the monuments of Istanbul and the clothing of Turkey. All four of us gape at the pictures while he tries to answer our questions.

"Are those minarets, those tall, narrow towers? Won't they break? Why don't they build them square-shaped like ours? The sultan's palace looks huge. Did you say there are hundreds of rooms? That's impossible . . .

"Heavens, their women wear jackets and bouffant pants, like men! Isn't that indecent? That tall white headdress that covers everything except their eyes is really strange; it's like heads of Tuareg warriors on top of midget bodies. And those wooden, high-heeled mules; it can't be easy to walk perched up on those things. Do Turkish women walk from rooftop to rooftop like us?

"What huge turbans! How much time does it take for a man to wind such a long length of cloth around that funny pointed hat?

"So that's what ships look like. . . . You say the oars are operated by rows of prisoners chained to the deck? Is the Tripoli port as big and beautiful as this one?"

My father has already told us about Istanbul, where he has been twice. But it's very different to see the pictures with one's own eyes, the colors, silhouettes, the living shadows, almost, of reality.

We are so absorbed by the illustrations that it takes us a while to notice the written part of the book isn't in Arabic, but in printed characters we don't know at all. Why is this? Aren't the Turks Moslems like us? Yes they are, my father replies patiently, and their language is printed in Arabic characters. But this book was written in Italian, by Venetian tradesmen who do business with the Ottoman Empire. He has to confess he can't make heads or tails of this writing, which is read in the opposite direction from ours, from left to right.

"I think this is like our *alif*," he says, putting his finger on a much larger character than the others, a kind of point that widens at the bottom, and whose legs are held together by a crossbar as straight and rigid as the blade of Jasim's dagger.

I remain completely silent. There are so many things in the world, and I'll only get to know a minute part. Ghadames, which seemed huge to me till now, is actually tiny—a few dried-mud houses surrounded by palm trees.

"And what about you, Malika?" my father asks me gently. "Don't you want to know what gift I brought you?"

He takes out a long, thin object from the bottom of the basket, wrapped in a dark green, soft leather case with little gold motifs. When I see the care with which he handles it, I understand it is a rare and costly thing, possibly the most beautiful gift of this trip, and my heart starts beating fast. When he finally pulls out the object, I am disappointed. All I see is a dark metal tube, wide on one end and narrow on the other. What purpose can it possibly serve?

"It's called a telescope," says my father proudly. "Ship captains use it at sea to spot the ships they want to attack, or to look over the details of their military defense, or to inspect the ports where they plan to take refuge. See how it enlarges things!"

He shows us the two glass lenses at either end. The larger end is rounded outward. The shape of the glass, he explains, and its perfectly smooth surface, enable human beings to see farther than nature intended. He urges me to hold up the narrower end of the instrument to my right eye. What a surprise! The details of the little glass painting hanging on the upper part of the wall—a painting that has always intrigued me because my mother says it represents an angel—suddenly jump in front of my face. Details like the angel's languorous eyes, the crown on his black hair, the folds in his long, flowery tunic floating in the sky, everything is visible with unbelievable clarity, whereas before all I could see were colored curlicues.

Then I focus the telescope on Jasim, scowling on the last step of the stairway near the rooftop. I am quick enough to catch his pouting, vexed expression, and even the tears in the corners of his eyes. He turns his head away, but too late. He's jealous, upon my word, jealous of my gift!

"Tonight, we can look at the stars together," says my father in a soothing voice. Then, for the benefit of my brother, who is still sulking, he adds, "After all, isn't it only fair that a girl who is restricted to the top of the house by our customs should be able to follow the paths of the stars in the sky with her eyes?"

I am waiting behind one of the pointy corners of the roof for the sun to set. The shadows are getting longer on the lower part of the rooftop. All around me the houses of Ghadames, with their pointy horns, seem pressed close together, like a large motionless herd.

The sky has turned my favorite colors, blue and gold; the birds are flying toward the gardens, their wings rustling.

I feel my heart bursting with joy in the presence of so much beauty. My father has stopped at the top of the stairway by the kitchen, where Bilkisu is fanning the fire for the evening meal.

At this hour, in their flowing gowns, the women have turned into nearly invisible silhouettes, so that once the sun has set, the men can go out on the rooftops again. My father unrolls his esparto mat, turns toward the east and says his evening prayer.

Then he climbs up the three steep steps leading to the highest part of the rooftop, the narrow platform above the storeroom, where I am sitting. This is where my brother and I used to sleep at night in the summer, before being separated because of our age, and it is the best spot for looking at the stars.

"We live in a perfect city," says my father. "Our ancestors created it out of very simple things—water and earth, sun and shade, palm trees and desert stones. This is why they attained perfection."

I smile at him. "It's true. I've never felt it as strongly as tonight," I say.

"I am glad you feel it. You must always remember it, for it won't stay the same forever."

"Our city won't stay the way it's always been?"

"No," says my father gently. "Cities are like human beings; they develop, they change, they die. You'll notice it soon enough, little Malika, though you're not so little anymore."

I understand then that my mother has spoken to him, and I stiffen. I already see myself as the bride, wearing the heavy jewelry for the wedding celebrations, and being told to stay still while makeup is applied to my eyes, cheeks and hands, reddened with henna. Papa must have sensed my recoiling, for he adds quickly:

"Your mother tells me you want to learn to read now. I am very pleased. Tomorrow, we'll look for a teacher who'll come give you lessons at home."

I feel a thrill of joy, but I can't help thinking of Abdelkarim. For a moment I am tempted to tell my father everything, to relieve my conscience and for the pleasure of talking about him. I know that Abdelkarim would have liked my father. But would my father have liked him?

Instead, I stammer, sounding fearful.

"W-w-won't this make the city gossip? People often say educated women don't make good wives."

"You sound like Meriem, that's how she used to talk," says my father in a gently mocking tone. "Only weak men are afraid of a woman who can read! But maybe *you're* afraid? Perhaps the fear of not finding a husband is stronger than your desire to read?"

"No, no! Don't think that for a minute! I really want to learn."

My father nods. I can hardly see him now that it has become completely dark.

"Don't worry. You'll learn and you'll find a husband, because the times are changing—this I know—and change will even come to Ghadames, despite its walls. Our city is very old, but after all, the Romans came here, and the Arab conquerors, and travelers from the northern mists.

"The only thing that never changes," he says, raising his head, "are the stars and the way they move across the sky. Look, summer is approaching. You can see the Vega triangle more clearly: the Eagle-swooping-down-on-its-prey, Deneb the Swan, and Altaïr the Soaring Bird. And that great constellation that we call the Caravan, but which some other people call the Chariot."

I listen and I daydream. . . . The moon has risen, chipped in a corner, its face thinner. Only a few nights ago, it was full and lit up the strange celebration in the palm grove. But that was a long time ago! Where is Abdelkarim now, on what roads? Later, with the metal and glass tube my father brought me, we will be able to examine the face of the moon and look at stars that can't be seen by the naked eye.

But I am thinking of something else.

With this tube, you can also see far into the distance in broad daylight. Who knows? With a bit of patience my vision will become more acute than an eagle's and I'll be the first to spot the silhouette of that traveler returning to Ghadames. Even before the lookout women posted near the city walls, I'll see his powdery silhouette floating in a heat haze far away in the distance.

Author's Note

Malika's story, which takes place at the end of the nineteenth century, is imaginary. But the city of Ghadames is not; it is in southern Libya, near the Algerian and Tunisian borders.

For the past twenty years the residents of the city have been living in modern houses built for them by the government. Their customs have completely changed as a result. Men and women mingle much more, and all the little girls go to school, just like the boys.

However, the Ghadamsi remain very attached to the old part of their city. I am greatly indebted to the people who guided me around the labyrinth of the old alleyways, opened their houses to me, and described their childhoods on the rooftops.

About the Author

A French journalist based in Vienna, Joëlle Stolz reports for *Le Monde* and Radio France Internationale. *The Shadows of Ghadames* is her first children's novel.